SHE HAS my heart

Printed in Australia

Cover and internal design by Shawline Publishing Group Pty Ltd

First printing: September 2020
This edition: November 2023

Shawline Publishing Group Pty Ltd
www.shawlinepublishing.com.au

Paperback ISBN 978-0-6488-2765-8
eBook ISBN 978-0-6488-2768-9

Distributed by Shawline Distribution and Lightning Source Global

A catalogue record for this work is available from the National Library of Australia

SHE HAS
my heart

BEVERLY HUNT

CHAPTER ONE

Sophie

'Since when did you become interested in art?' I place the invitation down on the bench where Hugo had thrown it when he'd stomped in from work earlier. *Men.* 'And why do you suddenly want to go to an art show? We've been married for twenty-odd years and you've never once shown the slightest bit of interest in art,' I can't help the regret that creeps into my tone. 'Why the change? It's just odd.' I mumble the last bit to myself more than Hugo, my arms crossed. When I realise this, I relax and drop my arms, hoping Hugo hasn't picked up on my mood. It's bad enough my voice has a tone but my body language is just rude. Hugo always says I have an aggressive tone when I talk to him. I think he's being petulant; he would disagree; we often do.

'Why are you being like this? I do something nice and you're critical. I can't win,' Hugo says with a swift shake of his head 'Our company did a warehouse conversion for this group. They own a few places around town and we tendered to them. They liked the changes and got us to do the work. They threw a few tickets our way as a thank you.' His voice is abrupt, angry.

'Nothing fucking odd about it. I thought you'd like to see a place I designed, not to mention the fucking art that I knew you'd like.'

I back down. 'That would be lovely, when is it?' He has never hit me but when he raises his voice I worry he will cross that boundary and one day lash out.

'It's Friday night,' Hugo mutters as he grabs a beer from the fridge. The more I think about it, it was a lovely gesture. I can get so annoyed and angry with him some days and then on other days feel like I'm on tenterhooks, never knowing when he will fly off the handle.

Pouring a glass of wine I settle in front of the television, but I'm not listening to what's on, adrift in contemplation. Hugo and I have our own particular seats, always the same. Sometimes it feels like we're in our eighties, not our forties. Predictable, we are so predictable.

Is this all there is to life? My life is dashing past on a downhill trajectory. *Does it get any better than this, or is this all there is?* I'm restless, bored. If I'm honest, I've been wanting more for some time now, but I have no idea how to get myself out of this funk. My middle finger traces the rim of my wineglass as I stare into it.

At forty-four, I'm healthy and content, most times, and my children are happy overall. I think I give them a pleasant home life; I drive them where they want and give them as much freedom as they can handle without getting into trouble. I laugh and joke with them, but do they feel the tension between their father and I?

I love my job, mostly. Juggling the professor's schedule fulfils and challenges me. He's a professor of mathematics, an absolute genius, a gentleman, and a great boss. But he lives in his own world. If his schedules aren't written down, he is thrown as to where he should be. It's like having a third child, or fourth child, if you count Hugo. Married to Hugo for twenty-two years, this is what I signed up for.

It took me close to five years to fall pregnant. The first time I miscarried at six weeks I didn't even realise I was pregnant, till I had what I thought was a painful and heavy period, which were always erratic and never regular. After a visit with my doctor and a positive pregnancy test, he informed me that even though I had miscarried, the hormones were still in my body. I had drifted out of the doctor's surgery in a blur, only noticing those around me when bumping into them. Some were aggressive in their tone. 'Watch where you're going lady.' Others were more compassionate when they saw tears rolling down my cheeks. 'Are you okay? Can I help you; you look upset?' Unable to speak, I nodded and kept walking. It felt like the world was running past while I was in the slowest of slow motions.

Aren't women supposed to know when they are pregnant? How did I not know? Maybe I'm not maternal enough to have children and I'm just doing this for Hugo? My thoughts are ingrained in my memory, along with the little soul I lost. I never told Hugo, knowing he was as desperate as I was for a family.

The miscarriage dwelt in my mind for a long time, feeling I had let us down. I struggled through my grief on my own, crying alone in the shower every morning under the cascading water. Then I'd put on my make-up and walk out with my made-up, happy face. No one ever knew, no one ever will.

Four months later I fell pregnant again. This time I realised. The signs were there; tender breasts, nausea and vomiting, often in the afternoon at work. The girls in the office joked that I was pregnant. I would smile but underneath I was frightened. I didn't want to know. I would go into a mini panic at the thought, afraid of losing this one too; afraid of telling Hugo about the first pregnancy, of hurting him. I remember thinking more about him than dealing with my loss. I didn't want him to feel the pain I felt. The pregnancy test I bought from the pharmacy sat in my bag for a week before I built up the courage to do the test. I was afraid to feel excited, to hope. Further into the pregnancy, excitement grew. *It will be okay; it's been eight weeks now.*

As we ate breakfast at a cafe one morning, Hugo made a remark about how much I was eating. I stopped with the spoon halfway towards my mouth and said, 'I think I might be pregnant.' I didn't feel scared, or jinxed when I said it. It was a relief to finally say it out loud.

Hugo raced round to my side of the table and got down on his knees, much to my embarrassment.

I heard someone whisper, 'Look, he's proposing.' I held up my wedding band to them and shook my head, turning the colour of a beetroot. I whispered to him to sit back in his chair.

He was so excited and attentive during both my pregnancies, and over the moon when Emily arrived. He would nurse her for hours, just watching her sleep, or talking to her. I gave up telling him to put her in the cot. 'Most of all I want you to be happy, because I am so happy you are here. I am so blessed to have you here, with Mummy and me, your Daddy. Yes, I'm your Daddy,' he would say. Sometimes I swear she understood every word.

When Adrian was born, Hugo had tears in his eyes. 'We're complete. He's perfect. We're perfect. There is nothing else

I want or need. I love you so much Sophie. Thank you,' he whispered to me as a sob escaped his throat.

For the first few months after the children arrived, I never got up to either of them through the night. Hugo would be the first one to wake and hear their cries. He'd bring them into me to be fed and put them back in their room when they were settled. He never complained and would sit in the rocking chair till he knew they were fast asleep, then put them in their cot.

When had we drifted apart?

Hugo's voice snaps me back to reality. 'Sophie. Would you like another wine? I'm getting myself a beer.'

'Thank you, Hugo but no, I might head up to bed. Goodnight.' Lying in bed, I wonder where it all went so wrong; are all couples are like this? Coasting along, leading separate lives without realising it.

I pick up my book and read, hoping to switch my brain off.

Annie

Jared and I arranged one of our lunch dates. Usually, we try to meet for lunch at least once a week, if our schedules match. But we can go months without seeing each other and though it's an old cliché, we will meet up months later and the conversation will flow as easily as if we had seen each other only the day before. No awkwardness, no bitterness that we haven't been around a great deal.

We notice each other as we approach our favourite cafe from opposite directions, smiling and greeting one another with a kiss on the cheek. We both have impeccable timing, neither of us liking tardiness. In one fluid movement Jared opens the door and ushers me into the delicious aromas of ground coffee and baked goods.

I love this place. Brick walls cover two sides of the cafe, balanced by floor to ceiling windows which allow natural light to filter into the space. The cathedral ceiling gives a spaciousness to the place, yet it remains cosy and warm with the lights that hang from the crossbeams.

Candice, our young waitress, greets us with the warmth of an old friend. We have been coming here for years and she directs us to our regular table where the chairs are so comfortable yet far enough removed from the other tables for our privacy.

'Thank you, Candice.' I'm never sure if she's heard me, as per usual, she hasn't taken her eyes off Jared. For a few seconds her gaze is held by him as if she is in a trance, hypnotised by his emerald green eyes with a Celtic twinkle that could charm anyone into doing anything. His mousey-blonde hair is perfectly mussed, but despite its casual appearance, I know Jared has spent a lot of time and an enormous amount of hair product to get his couture cut just perfect. I think it's the only thing that Jared gets just right; his hair. He tells me it's like a ritual, a meditation to him and the bigger the case he has, the longer he spends on his hair. Not out of vanity, but to relax him and allow him to run through the case before he goes into court.

'Hello Annie,' Candice acknowledges me. 'Hello Jared,' she says, a blush spreading across her cheeks at his name. 'Coffee to start?' I thank her and she disappears with a nod to give our order to the barista.

Jared steps behind me and holds out my chair, something

he has done for as long as I can remember, no matter if we were in a small cafe like this or a five-star restaurant. After I'm seated, he moves around to his chair and sits down. 'I want you to come with me to the opening of the art exhibition,' he says. 'You have to come with me. I want you there, please, this is important to me.'

'Why? I know nothing about art, and it sounds pretentious,' I reply, picking up the menu out of habit. I know the menu off by heart and most days order the same thing, unless one of their specials takes my fancy. I give him a brief glance over my reading glasses.

'Please come.' Jared continues to look at me with those big green twinkling eyes. 'If I'm wrong about him, I'll have you there as my date so I won't look so desperate.'

'You could never look desperate Jared. Cool, yes. Desperate, no. And besides if I come as your date, it will look like you've bought your mother,' I say.

'You don't look that old, darling. Besides, it would honour me to have you on my arm. My little fag hag.' Jared tilts his head sideways, knowing very well he's winding me up.

'Stop calling me that!' I slap his arm in good humour. 'I'm not your little fag hag, your fruit fly. I'm a lesbian, and some days I feel old enough to be your mother.'

'Unless you started having sex with boys at a very young age darling, you are not old enough to be my mother. And besides, even though you were a late bloomer, we both know you were looking at girls at thirteen,' he said with a smirk and a wink.

'Not all of us are not so self-aware or perceptive as you, to think it was not just a phase as so many others do. You knew at fifteen, but you just wanted to be sure. You were of the opinion, as soon as you told your parents, it was real. You did two years of soul searching. I just had to discover it myself; or discover it on feeling my first set of breasts on the one we shall never speak of.' I laugh as I poke my tongue out at him. 'And by the way, twenty-one is not a late bloomer.'

I met Jared about twenty years ago when I was volunteering at a drop-in centre for gay and lesbian youth. The centre offers support, counselling and a haven where kids could come and meet other like-minded teenagers. Jared and I clicked from the beginning. At fifteen, he had maturity beyond his years, an old soul with a wicked sense of humour. He cared for people, often putting others before himself. At fifteen you expect kids to be more about themselves, but there was such a caring nature about him. Twenty years later his soul and caring nature hasn't changed. That's what I love about him, his passion and his insight, not just into himself but others also.

Jared came out to his parents before he finished college. He had done a lot of soul searching for about two years prior and wanted to tell them when he was sure of his sexuality and not just a phase he was going through. He needed absolute certainty that this was the way he was and the way he wanted to live his life.

Jared asked me to come with him the night he would tell his parents he was gay, for support. It was one of the most amazing scenes I have witnessed but not all families can be so welcoming and amazing at the same time.

His parents accepted the news, his father saying it wasn't a surprise given his caring nurturing side, even as a teenager. His father's primary concern was how society would accept him. Not all people are forgiving, his father would often say. Both men hugged and cried at the same time.

His mother just stood there, looking at father and son, silent tears cascading down her cheeks. She had her hands to her mouth, stopping herself from sobbing.

I walked over to her and put my arm around her for support. "Are you okay? You don't appear surprised by his news," I asked.

"I always knew he was special. I always knew he was gay. I'm just happy that his father is accepting it. That was my biggest fear when Jared came to the realisation of his sexuality, that his father would push him away. These are tears of joy." She smiled at me through her tears. I knew then where Jared got his smile.

Over lunch we fill the conversation with the upcoming art show, the artists involved; it would be the first time many of them had shown their art in such a sizeable space.

'How did the art show come about? How come you're involved, or how did you become involved in it?' I ask.

'The artists approached the firm asking for help and advice about staging their own show. As new artists they were finding it hard to show their work in galleries, so they took matters into their own hands and are putting on their own show. They're nervous about it. It needs to be a success, so they don't lose money. It's a big gamble for them, but they believe in their work, which is great. I admire their passion and the belief they have in themselves. It's my job to review the contracts from the gallery they have hired, for the artists, or for some of them at least. Marcus is one artist I'm working with,' Jared said. 'Annie, I can't wait till you meet Marcus. He's just an amazing, beautiful person. Inside and out,' Jared gushes.

'Tell me more about him. I get the beautiful inside and out bit;

but tell me more. Fair, dark, tall, short, skinny, not skinny? Come on, spill.'

I haven't seen or heard Jared like this for a long time and it's good to see the life back in him, the sparkle back in his emerald green eyes. Not that he ever showed how dark his world felt. During those bleak times I would just lie with him and hold him while he cried, sobbed, or just stared into space. This profound change in him brought a smile to my face. I couldn't help but enjoy his animation and happiness. I never want to see Jared in pain again.

'His name is Marcus. He's thirty-two, so three years younger than me. His parents emigrated from Spain years ago. Marcus and three of his siblings were born here, he's the youngest of five. Two brothers and two sisters, and they all have kids. He is Uncle Marcus to six nephews and seven nieces. He has black curly hair, loose curls… soft, loose curls.' Jared shows by waving his hands around his own hair. 'Olive skin and the darkest, biggest brown eyes; they're almond shaped with the longest, darkest eyelashes I have ever seen. I think he's caught me staring at him, and his eyes, they are hypnotic. He's a little shorter than me with swimmer's shoulders.' Jared gestures at his own shoulders for emphasis… 'And just a likeable person. He's not flamboyant, quiet like he's thinking before he speaks,' Jared takes a breath. 'I like him.' This last part is a whisper, as if trying not to jinx himself. 'I feel I'm in a tough situation. I need to be professional, so asking a client out is not on the radar. Plus, I don't even know if he is gay so that's even more of a risk.' His foot taps nervously on the floor, his leg slightly rattling our table. I steady my cutlery and Jared continues, 'The firm have had a few lunch meetings with the artists and Marcus and I would always end up sitting next to, or near one another. I don't seek Marcus out, and doesn't seem like he's seeking me out either. It always ended up that way and we would just talk. He's so easy to talk to and I need to remind myself we're at a business lunch, so we best listen to the boss. I do not want to get on the wrong side of Aaron. Did I tell you he's been made senior partner?'

'Yes, you told me last week.' I flutter a hand dismissively, not wanting the conversation to turn to Jared's uptight boss. 'I can sense how much you like Marcus. You phone me after every meeting you have with him. Going on about how gorgeous he is, how shy, unsure of himself as an artist he is, how modest he is. I've not seen you so affected by someone for a long time.' I smile. 'It's good to see you happy.'

'So please, will you come with me?' Jared said with all seriousness. 'It's this Friday.'

'Yes of course, I'll be there with you,' I said without a second thought or hesitation, wondering why I sounded gruff with him earlier when he asked me to come with him. 'What time do you want to be there? Work is horrendously busy, so you might have to pick me up from there. I want to tie up some loose ends so I can have a free weekend.'

'Can you be ready by 6.30? That way we'll be there by 7. The show doesn't start till 7.30 but I need to get there earlier.' Jared said, still a little nervous. 'You will be on time?'

'I'll shower and change at work. Besides, when am I ever not on time?' Jared's eyes narrow and I hastily correct, 'With that *one* exception, I'm always on time.' I wink, trying to put him at ease.

'Even I thought she was hot darling! I don't even know how

you got out of there alive. She could have turned me and I'm a gold star!' We both laugh as we remember back to the blonde who wouldn't let me go. Jared and his euphemisms. He loves telling women that he is a gold star when they flirt with him, asking him to come home with them. It's something he is proud of, having never slept with a woman. 'I know this is important for you and I'll be there, J, and I'll even be early.' When I shortened his name to J, he knows I'm serious.

CHAPTER TWO

Annie

While driving over to the art opening, Jared is fidgety and anxious, tapping his middle fingers on the steering wheel. 'JARED! Relax will you, you're making me nervous! And I'm not even interested in him,' I say. I soften at the blush in his cheeks. 'After tonight he isn't a client anymore, he is just someone you met through your work. Talk to him, ask him about his girlfriend, or if he has a partner, did he bring his partner? They're always good questions. Open him up a bit, if he's sincere, he'll let you know which team he bats for.'

We arrive at the former warehouse turned art gallery in plenty of time and meet up with the senior and junior members of the firm, their partners and some of the artists. I haven't seen anyone who resembles Marcus yet, but am introduced to Nikki, the curator of the show. Not that I could have missed her, darting around the gallery with purpose in her stride, eyes everywhere; on her staff and the paintings, adjusting several as she passes them, ensuring every detail is perfect. Combined with her long, red, curly hair and almost six-foot stature, she's hard to miss. The woman oozes calm, professionalism and a love of life and art.

'This is an amazing place you have here Nikki. I love it. The lighting is perfect, not that I am an art connoisseur by any stretch of the imagination. I've always loved old warehouses. They make great art spaces; they allow you to step back and appreciate the work. To get a real feel for it. Well that's what I find; I like to stand back from a painting and take it all in.' I feel like such a novice standing next to this woman.

Nikki and I discuss what it involves to stage a show. You can hear the passion in her voice as she talks and her enthusiasm is contagious…

'I know a few journalists that owe me favours. I want the wider public to know about it. The journalists will do write ups about what they think of the show so that shouldn't hurt the image of the artists either. The more people see their work the better. We just need to get it out there. I think all the artists are all so talented, and I'm so excited to be involved in it,' Nikki says.

'It's just incredible. There is a lot of talented people in the room. I should let you go. It looks amazing Nikki, you've done the artists' work proud,' I say, meaning every word. 'And lovely to meet you.'

'Thank you, lovely to meet you too,' Nikki says, striding off with purpose and efficiency in her movements.

Jared is occupied with his bosses from the firm, so I wander, happy to look at art on my own. I like it this way, I can take my time and not be rushed.

I meander around the gallery, stopping to chat with some of Jared's work colleagues who I've met at other company parties and the kids' Christmas parties the firm puts on every year.

It is a very family and gay friendly company. The company has represented a few clients in unfair dismissal cases when an organisation, upon discovery that the client is gay or lesbian, has dismissed them citing differing reasons but when challenged on those grounds, were unsubstantiated. The firm has an excellent reputation within the gay community.

On my way to look at another painting, I come to an abrupt stop; the hairs on the back of my neck standing up. My senses heightened, something I can't quite explain makes me turn around. As I turn, my eyes find her, ignoring the other people in the room, fixated only on her. I can only see the back of her, but something makes it impossible to look away. Is it her hair? I've always had a thing for brunettes.

It cascades just past her shoulders, with a little kick at the bottom. Is it the way her black dress hugs her body? Fitting her so well, coming to rest just above her knees. A perfect body. Not tall, but her legs were utter perfection. Four-inch heels stress her height; she'd be maybe five and a half foot, without them. To me she looks like a goddess.

My heart is racing. Butterflies flit in my stomach and I feel my wetness stir. *Settle down Annie and pull yourself together.* My internal chatter driving me crazy.

I can't turn away, don't want to turn away. I don't know for how long I've been staring when she turns. She looks over her right shoulder and straight at me, *into* me. I can't look away. I know I will never forget this moment.

You see this in movies, but it doesn't happen in real life, or so I've always thought. The world around us ceases to exist. The noise in the room fades away and it's just her and I. Transfixed, bewitched, and captivated. She smiles. And it's one of the nicest, sweetest, brightest, most beautiful smiles I have ever had the pleasure of witnessing. I smile in return and there's no embarrassment. Although I've never met her, never seen her before, I feel an instant connection to her. I want to protect her. Hug her. Hold her. Forever.

A man walks up to her and put his arm around her, claiming what was his, or that's how I viewed it. The smile evaporated from her beautiful face and she turns away. The moment between us had felt like it had stretched on for hours, but had only been seconds. I watch as she bristles under his touch and tries to shake his arm away from her. Her shoulders slump and his arm remains draped about her.

I wonder who she is? It doesn't matter. She is straight and not into women. Typical. Me and straight women. What is it about them? I sigh.

Sophie

As I stand chatting to Hugo's business partners, warmth radiates down my back. It's reassuring, soothing, and makes me relax. Where is this warmth emanating from? Waiting for a slight break in the conversation, I glance over my right shoulder, meeting the gaze of a woman staring at me from across the room. Her blonde ringlet hair captures my attention straight away. Messy but controlled at the same time. I can't peel my eyes away. Do I know her? It feels like I know her. My brow furrows as I try to place her. Failing that, I smile at her; knowing I should stop staring but not wanting to break the contact. She looks so familiar. The stranger smiles back at me, revealing sweet dimples and highlighting her high cheekbones.

I'm snapped back to reality as Hugo's arm slides around my waist, returning me to the conversation. Anger floods my body as he asserts his control. With reluctance, I shift my attention back to Hugo and what's important to him. Talk about going from warm to the other extreme in one touch. I shudder, trying to shake off Hugo's touch as I try and return to the conversation. One thought lingers in my mind: who is she?

CHAPTER THREE

Annie

Trying to forget the beautiful stranger, I resume my perusal of the paintings. I'm captivated by each one. The styles of the painters are so different. I stop at one painting, tilting my head from side to side. It's an abstract piece and the longer I look at it the more I find different aspects to it. It's mesmerising. Hypnotic. A sudden warmth engulfs me. A calmness I've never felt before. I sense something, or someone near me.

'Beautiful, isn't it? From any angle in the room, you get something different from it. You see something new. I love paintings that do that.' The voice is husky and sexy as hell.

'I was just thinking the same thing.' I turn, meeting the same sweet, bright smile I had the pleasure of seeing earlier in the evening. The bluest of blue eyes, which laugh and dance as she smiles, lighting up her entire face. This close, I can see her hair has a tinge of red throughout. 'It's so beautiful I can't seem to look away,' I say as I look into her eyes.

'Hi. Sophia Williams, we noticed each other earlier,' she says in *that* voice.

'Hi, Annette Mitchell, pleasure to meet you, Sophia.' I hold out my hand to shake hers. She takes it and she has the softest skin, with a warmth that radiates through my palm and up my right arm, the comfort settling across my chest.

'Please, call me Sophie, everyone does. Except my mother when I'm in trouble,' she gives a throaty laugh.

I laugh. 'Same here, I totally understand that. Mothers can still make you feel like a naughty ten-year-old who got caught with your hand in the cookie jar. Please, call me Annie.'

'Very nice to meet you, Annie.' That smile again. I could look at that smile and those blue eyes all day. She is even more beautiful up close. A sigh escapes my lips as I gaze into her beautiful blue eyes.

'I'm not boring you already, am I?' Sophie asks smiling and I can surmise she has a wicked sense of humour.

'Sorry. How rude of me, it's just been a long day at work and then rushing out to get here on time.' I give a sheepish laugh and blush, hoping she wouldn't think me an ignorant fool or worse, bored with her. I don't think I could ever be bored with her. *Annie! Stop the internal dialogue.*

We stand and chat with ease. Small talk can be an effort with some people, in particular upon first meeting, but with Sophie it's comfortable. We accept another champagne from a passing waiter. I think this may be the second, or third champers we've had since we've been standing here chatting.

'Have you come alone tonight, Annie, or did you come with someone?' Sophie asks with an expression I can't quite read. I wonder at the motivation behind her question. *She is straight, right?* 'Annie?'

'Sorry, champagne must be going to my head. I came with Jared, a friend of mine. He's one of the lawyers working with the artists. He did some legal work for them, he's here somewhere.' I scan the room looking for Jared and smile when I spot him. 'That's him over there, talking to the gentleman with the dark curly hair. That's Marcus, one of the artists in the show.' Nikki had introduced all the artists earlier, but I was unsure if Sophie would remember their names. *I hope she doesn't think I said that in a condescending fashion. She may feel I'm patronising her. Please don't think that.*

'Wow, is that his boyfriend? They look so good together,' Sophie says, looking at Jared and Marcus.

'He wishes,' I laugh.

'Well, I think something is happening there,' Sophie says, quirking an eyebrow as she sips her drink.

Looking over to them, I see Marcus saying something to Jared. He reaches up to touch Jared's upper arm and they both laugh. Their body language is saying a lot as they stand close together and Jared leans over and whispers in Marcus's ear. Marcus gives an ear-splitting smile. I smile. 'Yeah, looks like something's happening, I hope so. Everyone deserves happiness, and a bit of fun,' I say and wink at Sophie. *What are you doing Annie! You don't wink at her! You're having a nice civilised conversation. Don't ruin it!*

'Yeah, we all want happiness.' There is a hint of sadness in her voice. 'I think it's something everyone craves. Happiness. Love. Acceptance.'

As much as I want to get into deep topics with Sophie, this doesn't feel like the right time or place. I try and keep it light. We return to discussing the different paintings and styles of the artists. I find her so interesting, and entertaining. She laughs at my jokes, she gets my humour, and my sarcasm, as I get hers.

In the middle of our conversation, a man approaches behind her. A beer in his hand, he looks as though he has had a little too much to drink. It's the same man whose arm she tried to shake off earlier.

'Sophia, I've booked us a cab, it will be here in ten minutes, just letting you know. I'll meet you out the front of the gallery. Oh sorry, Hugo Williams, Sophia's husband,' he says and holds out his hand to me.

'Annette Mitchell.' I return his handshake.

'Out the front in ten minutes Sophia. Nice to meet you, Annette,' he mumbles with a little slur in his speech and a slight stagger as he walks away.

'I wish I could say the same thing, Hugo,' I mumble once he is out of earshot. I look up to see a smiling Sophie. 'I said that out loud, didn't I? I'm so sorry Sophie, I didn't mean to say that about a man I met all of thirty seconds, and your husband. I must remember to engage brain before opening my mouth. Again, I am so sorry.' I wish the ground would open up and swallow me with it. 'I'll just change feet so I can put my other foot in it,' I say.

'Don't apologise. He can be a real prick when he's been drinking, and we've argued. Not a pleasant combination I'm afraid.'

'I better let you go then. I've monopolised too much of your time already.' I don't mean a word of it. I've enjoyed her company more than I can remember enjoying anyone's company for a long time.

We stand there looking at each other, neither of us wanting to go, not wanting to leave each other's company. Damn it! I think to myself, what have I got to lose? I fish around in my handbag, finding my pen and purse and retrieve my business card. 'Here, call me. I've put my personal number on the back. If you just want to chat, grab a coffee, a bite to eat, please call. I'd love to catch up again.' *Oh, I would love nothing more than to watch you eat, watch how you sip your tea, coffee, whatever. Stop it, Annie. She'll think you're a psycho.*

'I would love to catch up again,' she says. She holds out her hand to take the card I'm holding. I place my card in her hand and close her fingers around it. I don't want to let go.

'Call me?' I whisper, still holding her hand.

'I promise.' She squeezes my hand. 'His master's waiting, I best not keep him.'

'Bye.' We say in unison. Sophie turns and walks off, losing contact with my hand at the very last second. She doesn't look back as Hugo guides her out the door to take her home.

Sophie

For the first time in a long time, I was happy for Hugo to make an appearance. If I'd stayed there any longer, I think I may have made a complete and utter fool of myself in her company. As it is, I feel a little foolish. *Annie. Annette.* I whisper her name. I've never been so drawn to anyone, ever. Male or female. I'm drawn to a female? Am I sure or is it just that I find her funny and interesting? Yes. There is nothing more to it. I love meeting new people… There is something about her though. Her confidence, without arrogance? The way she holds herself? I can't understand why I'm overthinking meeting this woman. I play with the card Annie gave me. Staring at it, still feeling the warmth where Annie held on to my hand. I can still feel where her hand was in mine and it feels so warm. Her lovely, soft hands; well looked after. She wore no nail polish, but the nails were manicured and cut short, with no hint of biting. I abhor bitten and tatty fingernails. It is obvious she looks after herself very well.

Hugo, already snoring in the back of the cab, is oblivious to everything around him. I hope I can wake him when we get home to get him out of the cab and inside the house. I'm tired of these drunken struggles with him; tired of him and his antics.

CHAPTER FOUR

Annie

Saturday drags by as I throw myself into work. I surprise the guys at the office when I turn up early and open the office, and on a Saturday morning. I try to keep myself busy throughout the day, to keep my thoughts from wandering to a certain dark-haired beauty with the smiling blue eyes; working late into the evening.

Running a small real estate business can be a little hectic when you're the owner. Everything falls on me and my employees rely on me. It's a small but loyal group of people and I find pleasure going to work, as we all gel and work well together. I'm very fortunate to have motivated people around me. They make my working life a lot easier.

When I arrive home, the house is spotless. I'd been unable to sleep the night before, so I'd opted to spend my restless energy by cleaning the house. With nothing left to clean, the empty house leaves me with only my thoughts to occupy my mind, and my mind is working overtime.

Will she call? Has she even thought of me? Was she just trying to make her husband jealous? Does she just want to experiment? Some women are curious, sleeping with a woman is just something they want to try. Never mind if the other woman is attracted to her, or has feelings for her, they want to try something different with no strings attached.

Once they've had their little jollies, they go back to the safety and security of their husbands and heterosexual lifestyle, only talking about their rendezvous when they've had a few drinks on a night out with their girlfriends. Is Sophie that kind of woman? Although, when I think about it, I realise that I never said I was a lesbian. I didn't think I looked like a stereotypical lesbian that night; I was wearing trousers, but I was wearing them with heels.

How would she know? Did she guess? Am I that obvious? Does she like me in that way? Maybe she was just being friendly, and I've misread the signs. Thousands of what-ifs go through my mind. I try to dismiss the irrational scenarios flying around inside my head. I select a nice red from the wine rack to have with the Chinese food I've just ordered. Saturday night. Chinese takeaway. *Rock and roll lifestyle, that's me,* I laugh.

Having fallen asleep on the lounge, I wake up a few hours later with my heart racing and my entire body in a cold sweat. I'd been dreaming about her; it had felt so real. I felt her kissing my lips. I touch my lips with my fingers, I felt her hands on my breasts. My fingers slide down into my panties. I feel the pool of moisture that has settled between my legs; that was some dream. She was here, it felt so real. My rational side tells me she couldn't have been here, but my irrational side is telling my body she was here as it tingles all over.

My dream of Sophie felt so real and left me aroused so I make myself come. But the orgasm feels empty, a quick release and usually I'm satisfied and relaxed. But tonight, tonight I want to feel someone's arms around me. Someone to hold me after they make me come. A single tear glides down my cheek as my orgasm subsides. Why am I so emotional? I've met her once and she won't call. All she was doing was a little flirting.

I finish what is left of the wine and head to bed. I take two painkillers and a big glass of water, hoping to ward-off the morning hangover. Another night of tossing and turning, another night of thinking. Another night of dreaming. *Let it go Annie. She will not call.* I succumb to sleep at around six a.m. on Sunday morning. I feel like I've been asleep for all of five minutes when I hear my phone ring.

The only early morning phone calls I get are work related. *Can't they deal with it themselves? And why call me so bloody early?* I pick up the phone.

Sophie

Why can't I stop thinking of Annie? Sitting on the sofa, all I can think of is her. Replaying it all in my head, every scene, going over and over everything. Her every move. That first look. It feels strange to me I'm thinking of her. She was splendid company, I enjoyed talking to her. I have met no one that vibrant, that exciting, that animated, that passionate, that interesting, for a long time. I could have chatted to her all night. This is all so alien to me. A forty-odd year-old woman sitting daydreaming like a schoolgirl; trying to wrap my head around all this.

Driving Emily to the cinema in a trance thinking about

Annie I almost went through a stop sign. I think if Em hadn't yelled at me, I would have gone straight through. I shudder every time I think of it, and what could have happened.

What have I got to lose? Will she think I'm weird? It's Sunday and perhaps it's her one free day of the week, maybe she likes her own time. I know I like my time and Sunday is the only time I can get it. Not every Sunday but some. I look at her business card and flip it over, dialling her number. My heart is racing at a hundred miles per hour and I feel sweaty. I hover over the call button for what feels like the hundredth time, maybe this is all too strange. It feels strange to me, all these thoughts and emotions I'm feeling. I take a deep breath, psyching myself up to call her and this time, I don't hang up before the call connects.

Annie

'This better be good and there better be an even better excuse why you can't fix it yourselves,' I say in my just-woken-up and not-happy voice.

'Annie? I'm sorry I woke you. I thought you would be up by now. Sorry. I'll call you later, after you've woken up. Please go back to sleep. I'm sorry. I'll call—'

'Wait Sophie, hang on. I thought it was work, please, please don't hang up. Just give me a minute to get my bearings,' I say in a rush. I want to talk to her, to hear her voice. 'What time is it?' Rising out of bed, I head to the kitchen to get myself a coffee and some much-needed water.

'It's 11:30. I thought you would be up by now.' There's a brief hesitation and then she says, 'If you're not alone I can call back later.'

'No Sophie,' I say smiling, 'it's fine, I'm here on my own, I had a restless night. Just settled late and had no idea what the time was. I'm sorry if I sounded gruff.'

'I hope everything's alright, is there anything I can do to help?' Sophie says and I splutter my water all over the kitchen bench. 'Are you okay? Are you choking?'

'No, no, no. The water just went down the wrong way, that's all,' I say. *Oh, Sophie you sure could help.*

'I was…' Sophie pauses for a second, 'I was wondering if you'd like to grab a coffee this afternoon? Maybe some lunch? But if you're busy that's okay. I know it's short notice, but we can make plans for later if you like. I know you must be busy with work, you've probably got things to catch up on. And Sunday is probably your only day off,' Sophie says, without drawing breath and I can sense she's nervous.

In a soft voice I say, 'Sophie I would love to have lunch with you. It would be great to catch up again. I know a great little coffee shop, it's totally out of the way and few people know about it. Or didn't. Word is spreading though. And the coffee is to die for! I haven't had a coffee like this since my travels to Australia. Australians know how make the perfect coffee,' I say. 'Will you be taking the tube? Waterloo Station is easy to get to from just about anywhere in London. It is just a short walk from there, down near the National Theatre.'

'The tube will be easier. Coffee to die for, you say? I am a connoisseur you realise,' Sophie jokes.

'What about a little wager then? If you don't like it, I take you out for dinner,' I say.

'And if I like it?' Sophie drawls, her voice low, exacerbating its huskiness.

'Well, I'm sure you will like it, you'll love it.' I smile into the phone. 'You'll think of something. You've got till two o'clock to come up with a payback.' We hang up after saying our goodbyes. I'm smiling. I'm jumping up and down. She called! She called! 'SHE called ME!' I say as I dance around. She called. She called!

Reality sets in. What am I going to wear? I don't want to look like I tried too hard, but I don't want to look like I didn't try enough. It's just a cafe. It's only coffee. *Relax.* It's lunch with a friend I have just met. A date? Did she just ask me out on a date? Is it a date?

Breathe Annie, just breathe. It took a lot of courage on her part to call. And she called me. She. Called. Me!

Sophie

Facing my open wardrobe, my heart is still racing and I feel flushed all over. I put the phone down. I can't believe it, I called her. I called her. She may think I'm stalking her. Has it been long enough? Maybe she was just being polite when she gave me her card. Perhaps it was just business, looking for a sale. 'Oh God.' I groan, 'What am I going to wear? What do you wear on a date? It's not a date though, it's coffee, a chat.' I'll find something suitable. Well, I think it's suitable, she may think I'm too suburban and housewifey. A poor, pathetic woman stuck with a bully of a husband and two kids. Maybe this was a mistake. Coffee. It's just coffee.

Did I just flirt with her on the phone?

I throw myself on the bed face down, 'What am I doing?' She may think I'm bisexual and want to play around? No. She never even said anything about being a lesbian. 'What the fuck am I doing?' George, my basset hound, looks up at me, drools and yawns. 'Thanks for the support, George.'

CHAPTER FIVE

Annie

After going through my wardrobe and trying on what feels like a hundred different outfits I settle on a casual outfit, but not too casual; hoping not to look as if I've tried too hard. The rejected outfits litter the bed and floor, they can wait till I get home. *I'm forty-two years old, why do I feel like a schoolgirl? Do we ever lose the nervousness of a first date? Is it a date? It's just coffee.*

True to my nature, I arrive with plenty of time. I eye Sophie as I come around the corner. She's standing outside the cafe, and appears fidgety, straightening out her skirt almost continuously. She glances at her phone every couple of seconds. *Maybe this isn't such a good idea.* She turns and sees me and immediately puts her phone back in her bag, appearing to relax. There's that smile, the one that lights up her entire face and makes her blue eyes dance.

Sophie

I'm early, why do I always have to arrive before time? I'm never late. Hugo doesn't like it. *We've got plenty of time, why are you always stressing about time? If we're five minutes late no one will notice.* This isn't about Hugo today; this is about me; I'm doing this for me. She's not here yet. Perhaps it was a mistake. How long do I wait before I go? Is she always late? I look at my watch and realise she isn't late; I've still got fifteen minutes before I need to worry. Although I haven't stopped worrying since I called her this morning. What possessed me to call her? I'm fidgeting, a habit of mine when I'm nervous.

I spot Annie coming in the other direction. She looks just as nice today as she did the other night. My eyes run from her head to her toes. I love the shirt she's wearing, bright in colour, paired with black jeggings, I think. She looks cool; I love her style. Converse shoes without laces; great look. She's here and she's early. She's smiling and looks happy to see me, that's a good sign, right?

It's a natural response for me to lean in and kiss her. I feel the warmth of her body as Annie steps closer to me and kisses me on one cheek then the other. My hand reaches up and I touch her arm as she leans into me. A sudden rush of warmth travels up my arm, which I find both comforting and relaxing. Annie holds the door open for me as we enter the cafe, even that slight gesture sets off butterflies in my belly and makes my heart beat a little faster. My cheeks are warm from my blush. The smell of good coffee brewing hangs in the air. Looking around, I can see why Annie likes this place.

Annie

I greet Sophie with a kiss on each cheek. 'Hello, I hope you haven't been waiting long?'

'No not long at all. I wasn't sure where this place was, so I didn't want to be late and keep you waiting. I hate lateness.' Sophie says and I smile. 'What are you smiling about?'

'I hate lateness too, it's a pet peeve of mine.' I frown as I say this. 'Jared and I are the same. It's like we try to outdo each other with being on time or how early we can be sometimes. A silly game with us.'

'How is Jared? How did he and Marcus get on? From what I saw of them on Friday night they seemed very content in each other's company.'

'Jared is well. He and Marcus are meeting for lunch today actually. Shall we?' I say and hold the door open for Sophie. We enter the cafe, which is deceptively large. Walking in from the street you'd expect it to be small, but it opens up and is quite a long space, with quirky little signs on the wall. I see Sophie looking around and reading some of the signs, smiling as she reads. I love the lights in the cafe. One is made of coloured bottles attached to a lobster pot with fairy lights hanging from the pot and between the glass bottles. I eye a new light. This one is made of small bike rims with old, pearl-like necklaces through the wheels. The owners are so eclectic in their taste and style. There's something new every time I come in; it's a funky cafe without being pretentious.

We sit and chat about everything and nothing in particular; righting all the wrongs of the world, but soon I need to ask the question. 'Where's Hugo? I thought you might have the whole family lunch thing happening today.'

'He sees his parents on Sunday. He helps his father around the yard, fixes what needs to be fixed and they have a Sunday roast. Sometimes I go, sometimes I've got too much to do so I make my apologies and get on with work at home. The kids always go with him. Emily, my daughter, has always been close to his mother and Ade, Adrian, goes everywhere his father goes. Some Sundays it's nice to have a bit of me time.' She pauses. I sense she wants to say something else. I keep quiet, hoping this will encourage her to go on. 'And... I've been thinking about you... a lot, since Friday night. I really enjoyed talking to you.'

I smile and answer, 'And I thoroughly enjoyed your company too...'

'Why do I sense a 'but' coming?'

'It's not so much a 'but', as a declaration. I feel I need to be upfront. I've been friends with women and further on down the track when a friendship has been established, platonic I may add, I disclose something and they pull back and the friendship dies. I make phone calls trying to arrange times for lunch or dinner and they always seem to be busy, doing something, kids sick, not pay week. And eventually I give up.' I put my elbows on the table, bring my hands together like I'm about to pray. I take a deep breath and say, 'Sophie, I hope it doesn't change things but you need to know this. It's a part of who I am. It's a big part of me.' I pause.

Sophie smiles. 'You're a lesbian. Gay. Whatever the proper PC term is these days. There. It's said. It's out in the open. Another coffee? You're right, this coffee is amazing.'

We both laugh. A good, therapeutic belly-laugh and the ice is well and truly broken. 'It doesn't bother you?' I ask.

'No, why should it? I like you for you. Your sexuality is not important. It's you, Annie Mitchell, the person not the sexuality that I enjoy spending time with. You're funny, you're interesting. I feel comfortable around you. I feel like I know you and yet we've only just met,' Sophie says as she lays her hand on mine.

'Thank you. I feel the same way about you,' I say. 'And how did you know I was a lesbian? I never said anything.'

Sophie winks, 'I've got gaydar you know.' Again, we both laugh, a little louder than what is acceptable as some customers turn to look and smile as they see us laughing.

Sophie may not fathom how important it is for me she accepts and understands me. If only everyone were as understanding. I think back to my best friend from school, we'd done everything together. Until the day I told her I had met and had fallen in love with a woman. Then the friendship just died. It broke me, tore at my heart. The friend that knew everything about me decides she doesn't want to know me anymore when she finds out I'm attracted to women? And then this former best friend and her two sisters have a night out at the only gay pub in my hometown? I was angry, so angry when I saw her, I lashed out. I remember saying, 'What? You've come to see the freak show? I believe that was one word you spat out at me that night. The night I needed to be accepted by you. Telling me I was a freak.' They left the pub not long after that and that was the last time I saw her.

Before long Sophie and I realise the staff are cleaning up around us and they have placed some chairs on the tables, although no one said to us they were closing. They let us sit and enjoy the afternoon, and each other. 'I think that's our cue to leave,' I say. I glance at my watch for the first time. 'It's almost seven, I hope I haven't kept you.'

'No! I've never enjoyed an afternoon as much as I did today. Thank you,' Sophie says, and I know she means it. We pay up and head out the door, standing on the footpath making small talk, neither of us wanting to be the first to say goodbye.

'I need to go. I've got an early morning meeting tomorrow,' Sophie says with a little regret in her voice. 'School lunches to prepare, you know what it's like.'

'School lunches? Got no idea.' We laugh. 'I'll call you,' I say.

With hesitation I lean in to give her a goodbye kiss on the cheek. Sophie pulls me into a hug and whispers in my ear, 'Thank you again for a splendid afternoon.'

'My pleasure,' I whisper.

We hold on for a little while. I find it so hard to pull away but soon we do.

'Bye.'

'Bye.'

With that, we both turn and head in opposite directions, heading to our respective destinations. I want to turn around, to catch another glimpse of her, but I keep walking. If I look back, I'll want to run to her and hold her again. I put my head down and pick up the pace to my car.

The afternoon flies by. It wasn't a one-off on Friday night. Annie is interesting and funny. I can't remember the last time

I have laughed so hard and had, without a doubt, a good, genuine, therapeutic belly-laugh. I didn't even notice the staff clearing up around us. I don't want to go, I don't want to leave Annie, but I have so much to do tonight before work and school tomorrow. Sunday nights are always the same. My life is the same. Same routine, nothing changes. Even family holidays are the same. We go to the same places every year. I should cherish the family holiday time, as the kids will soon be too old to want to go on holidays with us.

'I've never enjoyed an afternoon as much as I did today. Thank you,' I say with total honesty. We finish the afternoon laughing at something silly I said, Annie laughs with me, not at me. She doesn't condescend or belittle me with what I think is my mundane life. She has breathed life and freshness into me. I feel like the old Sophie when I'm around her. The girl I once was before another life took hold.

Annie leans in to give me a kiss on the cheek and I pull her into a hug. I want to hold her, to not let go of the embrace; but with reluctance I do. We're in the middle of a busy street yet I have the strongest urge to stay in her arms. I feel happy, secure, here. Reluctantly we say our goodbyes and I pick up the pace as I leave, not looking back. I daydream of Annie all the way home, smiling so hard my cheeks hurt.

Opening the door to the house, I am snapped back to reality. 'I thought you'd be here when we got back. Where have you been?' Hugo asks before the door is even closed.

'Hello Hugo, how are your parents? How was lunch?' I say, trying to deflect the question to give myself time to come up with an excuse.

'They're well, they send their love and they hope to see you next Sunday. They miss you Sophia, especially Mum. She had some crafty thing to show you and was hoping you could help her finish it. I'm not sure what she was on about, it just looked like a piece of material to me. Ask Emily, she sat with her and tried to help,' Hugo prattles on about the afternoon. I listen but nothing sinks in, still daydreaming about my afternoon. Lost in his recount, I know I have escaped Hugo's question.

Hugo finishes his monologue and heads to the fridge for a beer before settling in front of the television. At least he never drinks when he is driving, that much I'm grateful for. He would do nothing to hurt our children or put them in any danger. He was, and still is overprotective of them, more than me. When they were little, it was always me encouraging them to do things, challenging them. I knew they were safe; Hugo was more uptight and nervous. He is such a family man; he loves his kids so much. I admire that about him. But what else do I admire about him?

I'm lost in that thought while making the kids' lunches, trying to think what else there is that I still admire, even like, about him, when Emily enters the kitchen. She sits on one stool at the breakfast bar. 'You look different Mum, did you have a massage?'

I laugh. 'No darling, why do you say that? I had coffee with a friend.'

'I don't know, you just look… different. More relaxed, I guess. Granny and Pop send their love. Granny had…' Emily launches into a story of how she helped Hugo's mother with a quilt she's making, interrupted by Hugo and Adrian yelling at the television and the football match that was playing.

This is my family. This is my life. *It's not always bad,* I think as Emily chats about her day, her friends and what is happening at school this week. I smile to myself and think about how much I love my kids.

I send Annie a quick text.

CHAPTER SIX

Annie

Returning home, I prepare for the following week at work. An hour later my phone beeps. I check the message.

Thank you for a wonderful afternoon. I can't ever remember being so relaxed or enjoying anyone's company as much as I did yours today. Thank you again. Hope to see you soon. S xx

I smile as I read the message. I re-read it, and read it again, smiling the entire time. I respond.

Ditto. We'll definitely catch up. Very soon. xx

Monday flies by, I'm busy sorting out issues with tenants, organising maintenance and cleaners for some of the units we manage and it leaves me no time to think about Sophie. By evening, the exhaustion sends me straight to sleep.

*

'Good morning. Mitchell Real Estate, Annette speaking. How may I help you?' I say, minutes after I settle into the office Tuesday morning.

'Good morning darling, it's been a few days, fill me in over lunch,' Jared says with a smile in his voice.

'It sounds to me like you'll have more to say over lunch than me. Good weekend?' I ask.

'Lunch. Let's talk then.' Jared isn't giving me much to work with.

'Okay, does one o'clock work for you?'

'Perfect. See you then.' Jared hangs up.

He sounds happy. I hope he's happy. If his weekend hadn't gone well, he wouldn't be sounding so bright, would he? I would love for Jared to meet someone again. Someone who makes him happy. I'll find out soon enough how his lunch with Marcus went.

At lunch I find Jared at our usual table. 'So, how was lunch on Sunday? I know you've been waiting for me to ask. Spill the beans.' I joke with him.

Jared takes a deep breath, exhales and responds, 'It was fantastic, I thoroughly enjoyed his company. We get on well and he's a total gentleman. We have similar interests and values. He's more of a homebody than me – not really into the scene – and certainly not into the drugs. He enjoys the theatre, opera, classical music, music in general. He's different from the usual guys that hit on me.'

The more he talks, the more enlivened he becomes. It's a delight to hear him talk about his date and see him this smitten.

'He's always been into art, even as a little child he would pester his parents or siblings to take him to exhibitions that were on. He would search the art section of the newspaper finding out what was happening and where. I think with those big brown eyes he would always get his way. His whole family have encouraged him and support him. His mum still has the first painting he did. Has it framed and all, I think he said he was eleven or twelve when he did that? A proper piece he did in an art class his parents enrolled him in.' Jared finally takes a breath. 'But I've gone on enough about Marcus, tell me about your weekend. I'm sorry I didn't call you on Sunday evening. Lunch went on longer than I thought it would.'

'That's fine, my lunch date went on longer than expected too,' I say, trying to sound nonchalant about it and failing miserably.

'WHAT! You had a date. Why didn't you tell me? Not with that quiet woman, the friend of Patricia and Pauline's? The one that never speaks when you're around, just looks at you. That one? She's odd, and weird, and not in a good way. Please tell me it wasn't her!' Jared says, almost screaming.

'No, not her. A woman I met at the opening on Friday night. And before you start it's just a friendship, it will be nothing romantic. I just' I shrug, 'enjoy her company and I think she enjoys mine. She's nice… I like her, a lot. And I shouldn't like her the way I do.' I whisper, 'She's married, with kids.' I sigh.

'Hang on! Hang on!' Jared says, stopping me wallowing in my pity party. 'Brunette, black dress, fitted her nicely, taller than you, but she was wearing heels, THAT married woman?'

'Yes, that's the one. How did you know?' I frown at Jared as I place my coffee back on the saucer.

'Marcus asked me if I came with anybody and when I found you, you were in an intense conversation with her and he asked me if that was your girlfriend,' Jared says. I laugh. 'What's so funny?'

'Sophie asked the same when she saw you and Marcus together,' I reply, smiling at Jared.

Jared gets serious and asks, 'So have you called her back?'

I raise my eyebrows without answering. 'Call her,' he insists. 'Thank her for lunch, ask her to catch up some time. Like sometime this weekend.' Jared goes quiet and eyes me. 'She called you and asked you to lunch, didn't she?'

It was more of a statement than a question. I sigh and answer, 'Yes, she called me Sunday morning. I think she thought I had someone in bed with me. She was so sweet and nervous. I can't call her yet; it's only been just over twenty-four hours. I should wait another day, I think.'

'Ask. Her. Out.' Jared states, 'It probably took a lot for her to call you. Call her. Thank her. Ask her out for dinner. Drinks. Coffee. Anything! Ask her how she likes her eggs in the morning when she sleeps over.' Jared smirks.

'Okay! Okay! I'll call her.'

'When? When are you going to call her?' Jared says pushing the point, knowing me well enough to know I won't call unless I give him a definitive answer.

'I'll call her when I get back to the office. I'll message her first and ask when it's a convenient time to call. Happy?' I say, feigning annoyance.

'Very,' Jared says with a smug grin as he picks up his sandwich and takes a bite.

CHAPTER SEVEN

Annie

Returning to work after lunch, I walk into the office and Jean, the new receptionist, hands me two messages. I return the first call. She picks up on the second ring. 'Good afternoon, Mathematics department, Sophie Williams speaking. How may I help you?'

'Good afternoon, Mrs Williams, you may help me by having dinner with me on Friday night if you're free.' Holy shit! Where did that come from? That wasn't what I was going to say. Talk about a Freudian slip. Oh gosh. Talk about foot in mouth. *Shit, shit, shit. It's out now. No going back.*

'Funnily enough I was ringing you about the same thing. I've got an entire weekend to myself. Hugo is taking the kids to Scotland for a family reunion. They're leaving Friday afternoon, and I was wondering if you would like to come over for dinner that evening,' Sophie says, ever so calm.

A thousand thoughts race through my head. In her family home, his presence will be felt even though he won't be there. I'm not sure how comfortable I'd be there. No, I know. I would feel awkward. It's their family's space.

'How about I cook for you on Friday night. I'm sure you'd like someone to cook for you for a change. I should warn you I am a basic cook, after years of living alone I make it simple and easy. Though if I ruin it, I do have the local pizza shop on speed dial,' I say and hear Sophie laugh on the other end of the line. Oh, that laugh. That deep, throaty, sexy as fuck laugh. 'So, either way you'll get fed either by me or the pizza place. And if all else fails we can get drunk and forget that we were supposed to eat something.'

'Sounds wonderful,' Sophie says, 'What time would you like me? I'll bring the wine.'

'How about 7 o'clock?'

'Perfect. What's your address? That may help,' Sophie says with a brief chuckle.

I laugh along with Sophie. 'Yes, that would help, wouldn't it?'

Sophie

This is all too easy. Talking to Annie is effortless. Her return call was not what I was expecting, and it was so easy to say yes to dinner. She must like my company, otherwise she wouldn't have asked me to hers so fast. I didn't hesitate to accept the invitation to her home; the chance to get to know her better. That's what friendships are all about. Right? Releasing an enormous sigh that I had been holding since I got off the phone to Annie; I can't wait till Friday; I think to myself and realise I feel giddy.

Why do I have an underlying sense of guilt? It's just dinner with a friend. There is nothing to feel guilty about. I'm not doing anything wrong. We're having dinner. That's all, just dinner.

Annie

The rest of the week flies by. Sophie and I have only exchanged a few texts; I don't want to frighten her away or scare her by calling her out of the blue. It's not like I can call her up and say, 'I'm just calling you because I find your voice mesmerising. I could sit and listen to you all day.' *Annie! Annie! Annie! Get a grip woman. Husband. Children.* Home wrecker. Yes. That would be me.

'Bye everyone, have a good weekend. Paul, you've got the keys to open? If you need me don't hesitate to call,' I say as I head out of the office.

'Hang on there! Where do you think you're going? You never leave before six, and it's only four. What's going on here?' Maree eyes me with suspicion and taps the pen she's holding on her other hand as I blush. 'You've got a date, haven't you?' She points the pen at me.

'No, I'm just having someone over for dinner. And what's this, the Spanish Inquisition?' I say, but I'm smiling. 'I need to tidy the house and make something for dinner. And remind me again why I'm answering to you two. Three!' I say eyeing the new receptionist. I wink at her and say, 'Try and keep these two out of trouble for me this afternoon please, Jean.'

'I'll try Annette, but I'm not sure I can promise that,' Jean says as I look over at her. 'Sorry, Annie.'

'Enjoy your date, boss,' I hear Maree say as I open the door and the other two chuckle as I walk out.

Once home, I tidy the house, putting away the paperwork scattered on the coffee table and give the house a quick vacuum. There's not that much to do since Josie, my cleaner, was in two days ago. I jump in the shower for a quick freshen up and apply a little make-up. I put on my favourite pair of Levis and white tee shirt. No shoes. I love going barefoot on the wooden floors. I'm comfortable and feel relaxed.

The lasagne is prepared; it's such an easy recipe to follow and I've made it before, so I know it can't go wrong. Dessert. Done. I'll light some candles. No, maybe I shouldn't. She may think I'm trying to be romantic. She may think I'm trying to come onto her. Should I blow them out? Just turn the lamp shades on. *Yes, Annie, blow out the candles and just put on some lamps. You were calm five minutes ago. Settle! Stop over analysing everything!* I blow out the last candle just as the doorbell rings and I open the door to see a smiling Sophie.

'Hello, lovely to see you. Come in,' I say, stepping to the side to allow Sophie to enter.

'Hi. I didn't know what we were having so I've bought a red and a white wine,' Sophie says, holding up the two bottles in greeting.

Closing the door, in an automatic response I take a step towards Sophie and kiss her on the cheek.

'Thank you. The kitchen is through here, follow me. I thought we'd have dinner in there. The dining room feels too big for just two people, if that's okay with you?'

'Of course,' Sophie says, as I take the lead and head towards the kitchen. 'Wow! Great kitchen. You've made good use of the space. I would love a kitchen like this.'

Set out in a galley style, the kitchen a bit wider than a regular galley and opens to the garden at one end. The table is set up beside the floor to ceiling windows I'd had put in when I renovated the place. I also have a big old comfy chair up next to the wall where I can sit and read for hours.

'It was a dump when I moved in. It was structurally sound, but it had a great feel to it. Just needed some TLC. I fell in love with it. Let me just check the oven then I'll show you around,' I say, and pause. 'I forgot to ask, you're not vegetarian, are you? I've made a lasagne with meat in it. I've also made a dessert. I won't let you starve.'

'No, I'm not vegetarian, I eat anything and everything, unfortunately,' she says with a little sadness, pointing to her tummy.

'What? Why say it like that? You've got a superb body, give yourself a break. You work full-time so I'm sure running off to the gym after work may not always be an option for you,' I say meaning every word. 'I think you look great.'

'Hugo says I—'

I put my finger to Sophie's lips to stop her finishing the sentence.

'Let's not talk about Hugo tonight. No offence, but I don't want to hear what Hugo has to say, I want to hear what you have to say, you're the one I'm interested in hearing all about.'

'Thank you.' Sophie says, 'Now what was that about showing me the house.'

After showing Sophie around, dinner is ready. 'Sit and relax. Please,' I say trying to put Sophie at ease.

'I feel I should be helping, doing something. I'm not used to sitting and not cooking. Emily has always helped me when I cook,' Sophie says as she watches me fuss around the kitchen.

'You can open the wine and pour us both a glass. I think it should be safe to have a glass now most of the cooking is done. I've had many a meal spoiled by having wine while I've been cooking. Not a good combination, but always a good laugh. If I'm cooking for friends, they keep the wine away from me till I'm almost done. They laugh and say they'd like to meet a woman firefighter but not by my house burning down.'

Sophie laughs and hands me a glass of red wine. I take it and my fingers brush hers. Again, a warm sensation travels up my arm and settles across my chest.

I smile. 'Salute. To friendship.'

'To friendship,' Sophie repeats as we clink glasses.

I take a sip of the wine. 'Mmmm… This is nice. What is it?' I enquire, picking up the bottle. 'Oyster Bay Merlot. New Zealand wine. I like it. You have excellent taste.' I don't think Sophie is used to receiving compliments. She lowers her head and turns her head, blushing.

'Sit down and I'll serve dinner. Any chair is fine. If you think the table is too small, we can go into the other room.' I say, not realising how small the table is until now.

'No, this is fine, it's cosy, I like it,' Sophie says as I place the plate in front of her. 'Wow, this looks great and smells delicious. And all homemade. I am impressed.'

We finish the meal, and still haven't drawn breath as I open the second bottle of wine. Why is this just all too easy? 'Let's go into the lounge. It's warmer and a lot more comfortable,' I say.

As soon as I walk into Annie's house, I cannot believe how comfortable I feel here. Is that the scent of a candle I smell? Did Annie just have candles burning? Whatever it is, it smells divine.

Annie kisses me on the cheek and there's that warm feeling again. I feel aroused around her. I need to block that out. I'm a married woman. Not happy, but married, and straight.

We go into the kitchen and whatever Annie is cooking smells amazing. I look around trying to take it all in. Annie has a few cookbooks on a shelf beside the stove but none open to show she has used them for whatever she has cooked tonight. She has some last-minute prepping to do before the dinner is served and she tells me to sit down. This feels alien to me and nice at the same time. I catch Annie just looking at me when I'm talking. I'm not sure if her eyes have glazed over, or if she is interested in what I have to say. But no, she smiles, clearly listening to me. I mention Hugo and she presses a finger to my lips, silencing the words. I love the feel of her finger as she cradles it to my lips. I want to kiss her. I want to take away her finger from my lips and kiss her. I shake the thought from my head.

'I want to hear what you have to say, you're the one I'm interested in hearing all about,' Annie says and I snap back to reality.

Annie keeps complimenting me over the course of the evening and I'm finding it hard to accept, but she seems genuine and interested in what I have to say. I'm having a great night. As I get up to move to the lounge room, I lose my footing and stumble towards Annie. I think I've had too much to drink and feel embarrassed as I lurch. Suddenly a pair of secure arms are around my waist, pulling me upright.

CHAPTER EIGHT

Annie

Placing the dirty dishes on the bench, I turn to see Sophie stumbling. I reach out to grab her around the waist, pulling her back upright and close to me. We stand there, our bodies touching, staring into each other's eyes, heat radiating from her body as my heart beats faster, in time with hers. Her breathing speeds up, her pupils dilate. Gazing into them, I whisper, 'You okay?'

'Never better,' Sophie replies, her voice just audible.

My breathing quickens as Sophie's face flushes I lean in, and pause, ever so close to her sweet lips, giving her time to pull back. She moves closer as I tilt my head to the side. Sophie follows suit, and in slow motion our lips connect. I moan into the kiss as her tongue finds mine. The kiss is slow, unhurried. She tastes sweet, and she feels so good.

My hands grasp the side of her face as our kiss deepens. My whole body tingles. It heightens all my senses as my heart races. The kiss goes on… and on. We pull away and I try to catch my breath.

Sophie

I think Annie wants to kiss me, and if I'm honest I want it too. The waiting is agony, I know she is giving me the option to pull away, silently asking my permission. We tilt our heads together and kiss for the first time. It's the first time I have ever kissed a woman. Annie is so gentle and feels so soft. The kiss is unhurried, and Annie tastes sweet. Did I just hear her moan? That's a good sign. My heart is racing and the kiss sends flames racing through my body. With just one kiss and my life has forever changed.

Annie pulls away. 'I'm sorry Sophie. I don't know what came over me. I shouldn't have kissed you.'

'I'm not. I wanted you to kiss me. I've wanted to kiss you since the first time I saw you. I don't know what it is. But… I am so drawn to you… and it scares me… What I'm feeling. I… I… I'm having trouble understanding all this. What I'm feeling is all so strange to me yet feels so normal and comfortable. Just standing here with your arms around me is so… so… I feel I've lost the ability to articulate.'

Annie

We stand there, our arms around each other and our foreheads touching, content in each other's embrace. Sophie, unable to get her words out, rests her head on my chest. We just fit into one another. I don't know how long we stand there, but I'm not in any hurry to break the contact.

'I don't know what to do with these feelings. Where they fit into my life…' Sophie's voice trails off.

I kiss Sophie's cheek and take her hand. 'Come on, let's go into the lounge and let's not overthink it tonight. There's a bit of alcohol on board and tomorrow is a new day. With a clearer head you may not feel as confused and I don't want us to regret anything or be embarrassed tomorrow by going too far tonight. I don't want you to feel I'm taking advantage of you because I'm not… and I never will. Okay?'

'Okay,' Sophie says with a sweet shy smile and her captivating blue eyes sparkling.

Taking last of the wine, we walk through to the lounge. 'If we're going to have a hangover, we may as well make it a good one.' I hold up the bottle to the light to check it. 'There's not much left, may as well finish it.'

We sit at opposite ends of the sofa. Sophie tucks her legs underneath her and faces me. I sit with my legs outstretched on the sofa, facing Sophie. The sofa is long enough that I'm not touching Sophie with my feet. Many a night I've fallen asleep on here and woken up after, sometimes the best sleep I've had. The kiss forgotten as we continue talking about family, friends, travel, work.

'I can remember I was about twelve years old, and a bit of a tom boy. Scrap that I *was* a tom boy!' I say. 'My two best friends in the neighbourhood were boys. I wasn't into the whole dresses and dolls thing like the girls at school or who lived in the neighbourhood. I loved playing football with the boys. Always leading them on some misadventure. Climbing the tallest tree, always the first to climb up on a roof to retrieve a cricket or tennis ball. Taking a tumble when I was coming down from a roof or from a tree.' I pause and take a sip of wine. 'One day, I was sitting on the front steps at home nursing a black eye I had sustained while playing cricket with the boys. Silly mid-on, shouldn't have stood there but it saved the match! Anyway, my dad came out with a packet of frozen peas for my eye and sat down next to me. Out of the blue I said to him, "I'm never getting married and I'm never having children." And he just looked at me and smiled, and said, "If that's what you want, that's okay with me." I just knew I didn't want to have children. All these years later I have lived by those words. Never married, never had children. It's not something I regret or miss. Don't get me wrong, I love kids. Adore my nieces and my nephews; just adore them. I would give them the world and they know it. Friends' children, my Godchildren, I love them all. I just didn't want any of my own. What you don't have you don't miss.'

'But don't you want someone there to look after you when you get old? Watch your grandchildren grow up?' Sophie says with a frown.

'None of that is guaranteed. Kids might not stay to look after you. Your children may want to go overseas, leave, and have their own lives. I was never maternal enough to want children and I don't apologise for it. I just knew.'

'You and your ex never wanted children? You were together for a while,' Sophie asks.

'The subject came up, but that will be a story for another day. I've seen you try and stifle three yawns already. I think you're getting tired.'

'I am tired, but I'm just so content sitting here talking. Your house is just so cosy.'

Rising to my feet, I hold out my hand to Sophie. There's

that feeling running up my arm again. I pull her upright. She doesn't let go of my hand. 'I think you should stay. You've had too much to drink and you're not safe to drive. I'll lend you some pyjamas, and I have a spare toothbrush in my bathroom. I can't offer you the spare room as it's being redecorated and it's a mess in there. The sofa is comfortable, or you can share my bed.'

'You don't mind me sharing your bed?' Sophie asks.

'With you, no. Although the sofa is comfortable, I want to give you an option. I want you to feel comfortable.'

'I don't think you could ever make me feel uncomfortable. That's the weird thing, I've never felt so comfortable around someone so soon.'

Sophie

I'm not sorry. I've never felt more alive. Yet it feels so foreign to me, and yet so natural. We go into the lounge and sit on the sofa, sitting on opposite ends facing each other. I don't feel embarrassed about kissing Annie, in fact I respect her more because she didn't take advantage of me. Is this what it's like with women? They show you respect.

Annie is sitting telling me about her life, or parts of it and why she doesn't want to have, or never wanted to have children. I find that hard to fathom as I adore my children and could never imagine my life without Emily and Adrian. They are a part of me and I'm proud of the young adults they are becoming. Caring, nurturing, able to look adults in the eye and hold a conversation with them. They show respect to others and, in my eyes, Hugo and I have raised them to have perfect manners.

I am getting tired yet I could stay up all night listening to Annie's stories. I think Annie has noticed me trying to stop my yawns. I hope she doesn't think I'm rude, that she is boring me with her stories. I don't think Annie could ever bore me. She's so interesting, talented and dare I even think it to myself, sexy. She has a confidence about her without being arrogant, and that's a rare find. I want to stay up and listen to Annie as I am fascinated by her and her stories.

'You and your ex never wanted children? You were together for a while,' I ask Annie. She had been with her ex-partner for so long I'm sure the conversation would have come up at some stage.

'The subject came up and that's a story for another day. I've seen you try and stifle three yawns already, I think you're getting tired.' Nothing gets past Annie as she had noticed the yawns I was trying to hold back with failed discretion.

CHAPTER NINE

Annie

We settle into bed, talking a little before rolling over to sleep. Our backs to each other, I'm on the edge of my bed. I'm comfortable but trying not to be too close. I sense Sophie is doing the same.

After a peaceful night sleep, I wake feeling refreshed and not hungover as I had feared. I'm in that half awake half asleep stupor and I can feel her warmth. She is cuddled up to my back, her leg over mine and her arm over my hip, on my belly.

Sophie moans, 'Mmmm… this is a nice way to wake up. I think I must have rolled over in my sleep. I have to confess I feel very cosy.' She plants a kiss on my shoulder.

I pick up her hand, bringing it to my lips and kiss her fingers. I study her fingers. Her nails. Well-manicured and well kept. Her hand is so soft; I can't help but kiss her fingers again.

Sophie

I wake from the best night's sleep I have had in a long time; I can't remember having such a sound sleep, ever. I remember falling asleep on the edge of the bed. It worried me Annie wouldn't be able to sleep with someone in her bed.

Waking in a state of contentment, I realise where I am; I'm cuddling Annie! Still half asleep, I kiss Annie on her shoulder. She smells divine. None of that male sweaty morning smell that I get with Hugo or the morning erection.

A panic sets in as I comprehend what I have just done. Have I gone too far? At that precise moment Annie picks up my hand and kisses my fingers. I relax, realising Annie is okay that I have cocooned her and she rolls over and puts her arm around me. She kisses the top of my head. It's a simple gesture, but means so much to me. Hugo has never woken up and done that. I feel tears welling in my eyes at the thought. A morning cuddle with no sex. No hidden agenda, although waking up like this, I wouldn't say no to the sex. I feel aroused with Annie holding me. Just a cuddle. I've missed this intimacy.

Annie

We stay in the same position, neither of us wanting to break the contact. 'It is a very nice way to wake up. Sleep well?' I ask.

'I did. And you?'

'Considering I haven't shared my bed with anyone for a long while, I slept remarkably well.' Sophie goes to say something then stops. 'Say it. I won't be offended.'

Sophie is tentative but asks, 'You don't have women sleep over?'

'I haven't had anyone sleep over in a long while. After Jenny and I split up I went crazy for a short while. They would sleep but I spent most of the night staring at the ceiling. I wasn't comfortable with just anyone in my bed. The next morning I'd offer to take them out for breakfast because I needed to get them out of the house. It was wrong and I'm not proud of it. Last night was different and I slept great.'

'Are we going out for breakfast then?' Sophie says with a mock hurt tone.

'No. This morning I'm making you breakfast. How do you like your eggs?' Smiling, I think of Jared's comment. 'But first coffee.'

'I'm not sure I'm game enough to move, my bladder is almost bursting!' I laugh. 'Stop laughing!' Sophie says. 'I'm not game enough to move, let alone laugh.'

'I guess tickling is out then?' I smirk down at Sophie, kissing the top of her head again and move to get out of bed. 'Use the ensuite. I'll use the bathroom downstairs. And I'll bring us some coffee up.'

Returning with the coffee I place one on each of the bedside tables; finding a headband to tie my hair back. Sophie watches my every move. 'What?' I ask, smiling.

'I've never seen you with your hair tied back.'

'Bed hair. It's out of control.' I laugh. 'It's wild and has a life of its own.'

My hair is a blonde mess, always curly and frizzy in the morning. I need regular help from the local hairdressers and am constantly buying hair products to keep the frizz out and the curls in.

We enjoy our coffee amid lots of chatter. When we finish, we lie facing each other. My arm under the pillow outstretched, Sophie is mirroring me as our fingertips touch, playing. Why does something so simple feel so good? We exchange no words; we just look into each other's eyes.

Sophie closes her eyes and moans. 'Why does this feel so good? Intimate.'

It was a rhetorical question. Looking at her, her eyes closed, I lean over, remembering it's now a new day, a new day with no alcohol for us to blame. I can't help it, I can't stop, I want to taste her lips again. I want to kiss her. I move closer. My fingertips brush her cheek as my lips connect to hers. Her lips are soft and warm, and the kiss is tender as our tongues entwine. Sweet. Delicious. Slow kissing. Unhurried. We've got nowhere to be. No one to see. No one waiting for us. It's just us.

My hand moves down her back and slips under the top she is wearing. I want to feel her skin, her bare flesh that is soft and warm. I can feel her nipples through the thin layer of clothing.

Sophie stops, pulls away from the kiss, looks into my eyes 'Please… please, don't stop. Please… I don't know how to say this… I want… more. Make love to me, I want to know what it feels like.' Sophie blushes as she leans in to kiss me again.

I smile as I peel my top off. There is nothing more I want to do than make love to Sophie as she lies there with her mouth open, unable to take her eyes off my breasts. I reach down and take her hands, bringing them up to my breasts. She closes her eyes and makes the softest, drawn out moan.

Moving away, I stand next to the bed, never taking my eyes off her, and slide off my pyjama bottoms. Moving to the end of the bed, I crawl up never breaking eye contact, not uttering a

word. Grabbing the waist of Sophie's pants, I pull them down;
she lifts her bottom up to help.

'Sit up,' I whisper, and Sophie complies.

CHAPTER TEN

Annie

Moving towards Sophie I sit between her legs, my legs on either side of her with my knees bent up. I slide her top up over her breasts, over her head and place it behind me. Leaning in, I kiss her, my hands reaching for her nipples, playing with them, with the lightest of pressure. They harden and grow under my touch.

'Are you sure? If you don't want to go any further, or you're uncomfortable, please tell me to stop, and you know I will,' I say.

'Please,' Sophie says, in a breathless gasp. 'Please don't stop. I… I…'

I lay her back down on the bed, and kiss her again, taking my weight through my hands. 'I want to taste you. Kiss you. All of you. Everywhere. I want to kiss you here.' I kiss her forehead. 'And here.' As I kiss her eyelids. I kiss her cheeks. 'And I love kissing these.' Kissing her lips, ever so softly. I pepper kisses down her neck, across her chest. 'And I definitely want to taste these.' Taking her nipple in my mouth I suck, pulling back to flick my tongue across her erect nipple. Sophie moans at the contact. I move to the other nipple and mirror my actions, eliciting the same response.

'Mmmm… I think you like that,' I say.

Sophie arches her back, trying to force more contact with my mouth and her body on mine. She squirms beneath me. I lift my body up, just a fraction, to tease her. She groans, knowing what I'm doing, what I'm trying to achieve. To torment her, to tease her.

I sprinkle light feathery kisses across her belly, and down to skim my tongue across from one hip bone to the other. I kiss the top of Sophie's pubic bone, and inhale, smelling her sweet arousal below as I continue to kiss my way down to her toes. I kiss every toe. First on one foot, then the other. Eventually, I slowly make my way up, kissing the inside of her leg as I move along her flesh.

There is something about the space behind a woman's knee. It's sensitive, a delightful place to stop and let my fingers roam the area.

Moving, I pay close attention to her inner thigh. Kissing and sucking on the area, stroking with my fingertips. I think it's driving Sophie crazy. Her breathing has increased. I look up at her, never stopping my movements; she has her eyes closed and small beads of sweat have formed on her forehead. Her fists clench the sheets. I can smell Sophie's nice, sweet aroma that is all Sophie; I don't think I will ever tire of it.

I want to tease her some more, drive her to the edge, to the brink; I match my movements on her other thigh.

Sophie's moans grow louder, her breathing speeds up, and her hips move up, trying to contact my mouth. I tease her once more.

As I make my way over to her other thigh, I stop; unable to resist. With my tongue I start way down near her perineum and bring my tongue up past her opening, lapping up as much of Sophie's juices as I can, sucking, inserting my tongue just a fraction before continuing my journey, before I apply a little more pressure over Sophie's clit. I suck on her clit before I nuzzle into her pubic hair and move onto her other thigh.

'Ohhh fuck! Sweet fucking…' Sophie doesn't finish her words.

I kiss Sophie's other thigh. I can feel Sophie's hand on my head, urging me to return to where I was.

'No! No! Please… don't stop,' Sophie says in a ragged voice. 'Please,' she breathes.

In one fluid movement, my tongue is on Sophie's swollen clit. I feel Sophie's orgasm is close, very close. I sense she doesn't want gentle anymore as I suck on Sophie's clit a little bit harder and give it a little nip. I taste her, I want her. My tongue never leaves her clit, moving over her aroused, red, very swollen orb.

Sophie stills, holds her breath and arches her back as she takes a big breath, moaning as she exhales.

I feel her orgasm building, her breathing speeding up. Her hands have a fist full of my hair. She is applying pressure on my head. Reaching up with one hand, I tweak her nipple as she comes and comes hard.

Sophie cries out in relief as she releases her orgasm and lets go of me. I smile. My tongue still firm on Sophie's clit. I can feel her orgasm as it pulsates through my tongue. The orgasm subsides, and I lick up her juices. They have oozed down my chin.

Moving up the bed, I settle next to Sophie, who kisses me as she tastes herself. Sophie licks my chin and the sides of my lips clean, before placing a sweet kiss on my lips. Her tongue enters my mouth, and I taste her again, and Sophie tastes herself.

This woman is addictive.

Sophie

Lying across the bed, I try to catch my breath, adjusting to what feels like an out of body experience from what is the best orgasm I have ever had. My chest is pounding still, but my breathing is returning to a regular rhythm. I can't believe what I've experienced. Isn't it supposed to be awkward the first time you have sex with someone? There was nothing awkward at all. Annie knows how to kiss. I don't think I could have ever imagined how soft, how sensual it is to kiss a woman. A thousand thoughts, a thousand sensations are still reverberating throughout my entire body.

Annie making love to me makes me think this is what it's like to be cared about. It feels like she can't get enough of me. When she started kissing me from my toes and slowly moved up my leg, I was wet in an instant. I didn't know what to expect and I've never been so wet in all my days. So soft, so tender, my body responded to every touch Annie placed upon me. I never realised I could become this aroused. She has taken me to another level.

Annie moves towards me, snapping me back to the here and now. Leaning in to kiss Annie, I can only assume I'm tasting myself. It's arousing, a mixture of sweetness and saltiness. Suddenly, I'm overcome with doubt and embarrassment. Was Annie repulsed by my taste? She would have stopped if she was. Should I have brushed Annie's face with my tongue like that? I've never done this before yet everything came together as though it was a normal experience. Where did this come from? I allay my fears as I feel Annie's tongue entwined with mine, dancing with mine.

I could be in trouble here.

CHAPTER ELEVEN

Annie

We lay there in silence resting on our sides, facing each other. Just holding onto one another with our arms wrapped around the other. Our breathing returning to normal. I'm comfortable.

'Wow,' Sophie eventually says and I laugh.

'After ten minutes of silence, that's all you can say?' I laugh with Sophie.

'I thought I'd had orgasms before. I *have* had orgasms before, but that, that was… again, you make me speechless… It was just mind blowing. I've never… I've never felt such a connection before.' Quiet tears start to trek down Sophie's cheeks. 'It scares me. How one orgasm can feel so intense, so full of emotion.'

I lean in and kiss her; slow, sensual, full of longing. I want her.

Sophie's hand makes its way to my breast; unsure. I guide her hand over my nipple and close my eyes at her gentle touch. My hand goes up to Sophie's nipple, as I tease it, her nipple enlarges under my fingers. I close my eyes, enjoying her touch.

'I—' is all Sophie says, and I open my eyes.

'What? What's wrong?'

'I – I want to – I really want to, but – I'm not ready – I don't know if I can. You know – satisfy you,' Sophie stutters out.

In a soft, reassuring tone I say, 'Sophie, it's fine, I won't rush you. Maybe this was all too soon. I'm sorry, I thought it was what you wanted. Please don't think I did this just for my own kicks. I like you. A lot. But please don't feel pressured.'

'I feel so selfish though.'

'Don't feel selfish. It's not like that. I could have you again and again and still want more of you,' I say.

'Really?' Sophie whispers.

'Yes. Really.' I kiss her.

My hand floats down Sophie's belly, gliding down to find a pool of moisture, already built up again between her legs. My fingers slide into her opening, pumping in and out. Her walls tighten around me and she feels so good. My thumb finds her clit and within minutes she comes with a large moan.

'Fuck! That was quick. I wasn't expecting that so soon. I'm not complaining, it's just never happened before… Fuck,' Sophie says, still trying to catch her breath and sounding bewildered.

Just as I am about to say something, her phone rings.

'Sorry, I have to take this. Hello, Sophie speaking.'

I try not to listen to the conversation but she's lying next to me. Is it him? And if it is, how do I feel about that? I'm a little bit envious that he has her at home every night and doesn't appreciate what he has. I want her so much. To love her. To have her. To be with her. I'm snapped out of my own thoughts by Sophie's conversation.

'No, no, no, now's a good time. I just ran across the road, that's why I sound breathless.'

I raise my eyebrows at Sophie who slaps my arm. Starting to get off the bed to offer Sophie some privacy, she grabs my hand

and pulls me back down onto the bed.

'No that works for me. Five is good. I'll finish here and meet you at Janice's. Better still, I'll pick you up on the way that way you can have a drink.' Sophie nods. 'Alright, I'll see you soon. Bye.'

'I'm sorry.' Sophie frowns. 'I completely forgot I was having drinks with the girls this evening. They knew Hugo and the kids were out of town and thought I'd be lonely, and we arranged this earlier in the week. I'm so sorry.'

Trying to hide my disappointment I smile and kiss her on the lips. 'That's fine, although little do they know you aren't exactly lonely at the moment.'

'Shut up and kiss me.'

'With an offer like that how can I refuse the lady.' I laugh and lean in for a lingering kiss. 'Right. Up and shower, woman. I need to feed you before you head out with a bunch of crazy married woman, who get up to who knows what when away from their husbands!'

'That kiss wasn't enough, I want more.' Sophie leans up and pulls me on top of her, kissing me with passion. Sophie whispers, 'I regret nothing, just know that. Believe that.'

'I do. I believe you,' I say as tears well in my eyes. I clear my throat, trying to keep the emotion out of my voice. 'Come on. You shower, and I'll cook us something. What do you feel like?'

'It's not exactly breakfast time, but I feel like bacon and eggs.'

'Coming right up, with lashings of toast oozing with butter. So bad but so tasty. Now go and shower! I don't want you running late and speeding. Grab a pair of undies out of my drawer. Here's a clean towel and use whatever you need in the bathroom.'

Sophie wraps the towel around her, and I watch her walk into the bathroom before making my way downstairs to start on the cooking.

Sophie comes down twenty minutes later. 'I hope you don't mind; I washed my hair. I saw the hair dryer before I got in the shower. It's just easier than washing it when I get home. That was okay, wasn't it?'

'Of course, it was okay. Make yourself at home. Now sit. I'm almost done. Soft yolks? And I'll just put the toast on. There's a fresh coffee for you too.' We sit and eat in relative silence. I don't think either of us realised how hungry we were.

'That was delicious,' Sophie says, leaning over and kissing me. 'Thank you. I'll help you wash up before I go.'

'No, it's fine. I'll put them in the dishwasher. Don't worry.'

Sophie looks at her watch, and frowns. 'I really have to go. I don't want to. But…'

'I know. Have a night with your girlfriends. They're old friends yeah?'

'Yeah, they are. Janice I've known since primary school, we're best friends we tell each other everything. Well…' She hesitates. 'Almost everything. We've grown up together. Most of the others I met in secondary school or at university. We rarely catch up but I—'

'No buts. Go and have a night with your friends. There is nothing like old friends. It's fine. Please go and enjoy yourself.'

After numerous kisses, numerous goodbyes, numerous 'one more' kisses, Sophie gets into her car. I stand at the driver's side, my arms wrapped around myself. Sophie lowers the window.

'Thank you for dinner. And brunch. And coffee. And…' Sophie blushes. 'A great time.'

Her arm is resting on the car door, I reach over and put my hand on top and Sophie places her other hand on mine, saying, 'When will I see you?'

'Whenever you want to,' I say in a hushed tone. 'Call me when you're free, and we'll catch up. I won't push you; I know you're busy. Just call me when you can, when you want.' I pause. 'What are you doing?' She has her phone in her hand and I can see her pulling up my contact.

'Calling you… I want.'

'Just go woman, before I drag you back inside. And enjoy your night,' I say laughing. I step back from the car and watch her drive away. I watch until she turns the corner and disappears from view.

Sophie

I drive away from Annie's place feeling lost and lonely. I wanted nothing more than spend the entire day with her, and perhaps another night. The thought of spending the night with Annie had crossed my mind, but that was a fantasy. People sometimes say it's better to keep a fantasy as just that, a fantasy. Fantasy is always better than reality they say, but nothing, nothing could spoil this morning. Last night and this morning had blown me right out of the water. Never in a million years, could I have imagined what occurred this morning, this afternoon, I can hardly remember the time, let alone the day.

Have I ever wanted to sit up all night talking to a lover? I don't think so. We have so much in common and yet some of our views differ. Annie has done so much in her life. Travelled, volunteered in some of the poorest and remotest places in Africa; and has seen some harsh and tragic events while she was there. She said it helped shape her into who she is today. You don't need a lot and she's right when she says that. You can't buy happiness, and she's right.

I had forgotten about the plans made by the girls; I'd been so preoccupied by thoughts of Annie. I'd never envisaged what had happened, but I don't regret it. But I am married. Married to a man with two children. When I'm with Annie though I've never felt more alive; happy. A new thought creeps in and I tighten my grip on the steering wheel What if this is just a bit of fun for Annie; am I just a straight woman conquest? She's got what she wanted, she could forget about me now. The thought of that makes me sick. Was I just a conquest to her?

What the fuck am I doing?

CHAPTER TWELVE

Annie

Heading back inside, still in a daydream, I busy myself with cleaning up. In the bedroom, I laugh when I see the bed. These sheets need changing. Talk about smelling of sex! The entire room smells of sex. I wonder if men and women have the same sex smell? Why am I even thinking of that? Ugh!

No paperwork tonight, mindless television is what I need. As I make myself comfortable, the phone rings. Hoping, wishing, it to be Sophie, I answer the phone. 'Hello?'

'Why are you smiling when you answered the phone?'

'What are you talking about? I just answered the phone.' I laugh.

'No, no, no, you were smiling when you answered, I could hear it in your voice.'

'Oh Jared, I'm always smiling when I know it's you.' I hope I've saved myself. I don't want to disclose my morning, my night with Jared just yet. Again, I smile just thinking of Sophie and those sparkling blue eyes, her husky voice and her laugh.

'I rang to see if you wanted to come to dinner with Marcus and I. We're having dinner out. Marcus is taking me for tapas and we'd love for you to join us.'

'It's sweet of you to offer, but I just want a night in. I've been snowed under at work and I just want to have a quiet one tonight.'

'That's fine darling, I totally understand. I'll see if I can catch up this week for lunch. Although it may not be possible. Work. Busy. I won't bore you with the details.'

'So, it's going well then?' I say to Jared smiling.

'Yes,' he mumbles, dropping the volume of his voice as if not wanting to be overheard.

'I take it Marcus is there,' Jared murmurs his confirmation. 'So, I won't ask any more questions. Call me when you're not so busy. Have a great night. Say hello to Marcus for me and give my apologies.'

'Will do, darling. Bye.'

I curl up on the couch, falling asleep and waking to a different movie. I check my phone, and smile as I read a message from Sophie.

Just letting you know I'm home safe. Great night. The girls wanted to know what I've been taking. They were telling me I was glowing. I guess I had afterglow ;) Thank you again. xx

I check what time the message came through, only twenty minutes ago, and I text back.

Glad you're home safe. And yes, you did have a glow about you. Lol. Sleep well xx

I make my way upstairs where sleep awaits me.

Throughout the week, Sophie and I exchange the odd phone call. Sophie calls as she makes her way out of work. We text each other when we can, but we're both busy.

Saturday arrives, and I've taken the whole weekend off;

sitting out on the back deck in the sunshine reading the weekend newspaper at a leisurely pace, something I don't get to do often so it feels rather decadent.

I hear the phone ring inside. Bugger! Why didn't I bring the phone out with me? I stomp back inside irritated with myself.

Sophie

I haven't stopped thinking of Annie all week. Going over and over our night, and our day together the week before. Every time I daydream about that day, I am just a pool of moisture. I've never had anyone make love to me like Annie did. I've never felt so wanted and desired before. It feels like I'm a schoolgirl again, experiencing my first crush. Except this isn't a crush and I'm not a schoolgirl anymore.

Annie hasn't given me the brush off yet. My mind races into overtime, overthinking everything. The straight woman conquest has been done and dusted but nothing has changed. As far as I can tell, Annie is still the same. She doesn't avoid my calls and some mornings, actually *most* mornings, she's the first to send a text. I hope she doesn't think I'm not interested anymore. I hope she doesn't think it was just a bit of fun for me. My mornings are busy getting everyone up and ready for school or work. I usually don't have the chance to text her till I'm in the car and stopped in traffic and my mind wanders to the beautiful blonde woman with those crazy, wild curls. If I was just a game to her, she wouldn't be doing that. Would she?

I need to see her.

Annie

'Hello.'

'Annie. Hi, it's Sophie.'

'Hi Sophie,' I say surprised to hear voice. My voice softens when I hear her. 'How are you? This is a pleasant surprise.'

'I have to be quick. Will you be home this afternoon? About three?' Sophie says in a quiet voice, like she's whispering.

'I'm in all day.'

'Can I drop by about then?'

'Of course you can, I'd love to see you.'

'I'll see you then.' Sophie pauses and declares barely audible, 'I've missed you. Bye.' Before I can respond, she hangs up.

Interesting, I think, *I wonder if she's alright.*

Just before three, the doorbell rings, on time as usual, and I smile, answering the door to a smiling Sophie.

'Hello you. This is a nice surprise,' I say. Sophie steps in and I close the door behind her. She is yet to utter a sound. Reaching over, with her hands on either side of my face, she leans in and kisses me, her tongue finding mine.

Sophie pulls back. 'I've missed you. Really missed you.'

I tilt my head to the side and grin at Sophie, 'Have you?'

'I have,' Sophie says before she comes at me again. Feverishly kissing me, her hands are all over me. Before I realise it, she is pushing me in the direction of the lounge. Feeling the couch behind me, I pull Sophie down with me. She lands on top of me, never breaking contact.

Still kissing, breathless and panting, I undo the buttons on Sophie's shirt, reaching under her shirt to undo her bra.

Sophie stops and stands in front of me. She leans down

and grabs the front of my t-shirt and pulls me to a standing position. Toe to toe with her, Sophie's hands find the hem of my shirt and pulls it over my head.

'No bra… I like,' Sophie says grinning. Her hands go to my breasts and her fingers skim my nipples. I close my eyes, enjoying the touch. 'Wow. You're so responsive. I've never…' Sophie doesn't finish the sentence as her head dips down and her tongue finds my nipple.

Sophie stands up, flushed, breathless. 'I – I –' I pull back and look straight into her eyes, still seeing the fear and worry. She is unsure of herself as a lover.

'It's alright, it's okay,' I say, kissing her. Our kiss deepens, becoming more passionate. Sophie's hands are in my hair, down my back. My hands slide down to her arse and back up again.

I slide Sophie's skirt down, taking her panties with it. As her skirt drops, so do I. On my knees in front of her, I bury my nose into Sophie. 'I'll never tire of your sweet smell. You are so addictive.' I lower my mouth and tracing my tongue over her pubic area, my light feathery touch making her shiver under my touch. She steps out of her skirt and I rise to face her, finishing removing her shirt and bra. Desire courses through my body and I discard my jeans. Sophie looks at me with a slight blush on her cheeks. I take one step to her and kiss her. 'I want you so bad right now; you have no idea how much.'

'Show me. Upstairs. Now.'

I grin at Sophie. 'You are demanding, aren't you?' Grabbing both of her hands and pulling her into me. Kissing her, I start walking backwards, bringing her with me. We stop halfway up the stairs, and I push her against the wall, kissing her hard, feeling the moisture between her legs.

We eventually make it to my bedroom where Sophie drops to the bed, and scrambles over to the middle, making room for me. My lips are tingling from all the kissing. With my thumb and index finger I squeeze her nipple. She arches her back, forcing more contact so I squeeze her nipple a little tighter.

'Ohh, sweet fucking… mother of… Oh fuck…' Sophie mutters.

My hand skims down to her centre and I play just inside her opening where her juices are pooling. The spot is so smooth, softer than the finest silk. I close my eyes to feel more.

My index finger glides in with ease. She is so wet, so fucking wet. I pull back again as my finger glistens with her juices. Bringing my finger to Sophie's lips, I insert it into Sophie's mouth, 'Taste yourself. Taste how sweet you are. There is so much more where that came from.'

Sophie closes her eyes, tastes herself, and moans. Her tongue encircles my finger, sucking on it. Now it's my turn to moan, as I grind myself into her thigh for some contact.

Pulling my wet finger from her mouth, I trail it down Sophie's front, and insert it again. There is something about the index finger, it is much more sensitive than the other fingers, feeling and reaching to a place that can only be described as heaven. Closing my eyes, I feel Sophie's walls as they start to tighten around my finger.

We fall into a nice slow rhythm, in and out. In this position I'm at eye level with her breasts and I can't help myself. I want to taste and feel as much of Sophie as I can. My senses are in overdrive. Licking her breasts with the tip of my tongue, tracing around Sophie's areola. I love this change in texture. Sophie's nipple starts to extend from my ministrations. My finger and tongue are in perfect rhythm. Nipping at her nipple, driving her crazy, our pace quickens, and Sophie asks for another finger.

I comply, pumping two fingers in and out… it's getting harder as Sophie's walls tighten. Her cunt is so tight. In her groaning I hear Sophie say she wants a third finger. I squeeze a third finger in and keep going, no longer sucking her breasts. My free hand reaches up and grabs her nipple. I play and tug at it. My own juices covering Sophie's thigh between my legs. As I ride her thigh, I feel Sophie close to her orgasm, my fingers aren't moving as she is so tight.

I rub Sophie's clit with my thumb, using the lightest of pressure. I'm still grinding myself on her thigh, then with an almighty moan, she comes hard. Her orgasm pulsates around my fingers as she gushes, squirting her juices everywhere. With that, I come. I am still on her thigh as I ride out my orgasm, tweaking Sophie's nipple just to keep her going a little bit longer. All the time, my fingers remaining inside her.

As Sophie comes back down to earth, I move up the bed and lay beside her, my fingers still buried inside. Ever so slowly, and I remove my fingers and lick them clean. Her taste is addictive. A sweet, delectable taste. One that I think I can never get enough of.

'Kiss me,' I whisper.

CHAPTER THIRTEEN

Annie

Waking to our entangled limbs, and a strong urge to pee, Sophie must have read my thoughts. 'I really need to whiz.'

'Whiz! I haven't heard that word in years!' I laugh, climbing out of bed taking Sophie's hand. 'Come,' I whisper as I lead her into the bathroom. 'Sit,' I instruct. Sophie eyes me in curiousness and does what I ask. I straddle Sophie's legs.

'Don't pee.' I purr as I reach down and open Sophie's clit to the cool air. I look into Sophie's eyes, wanting to see her expression of surprise. I pee as Sophie's eyes widen. Her mouth opens but nothing comes out. Sophie closes her eyes. The feeling of a warm fluid cascading over her clit as I pee, her clit exposed to the air. Her mouth opens and closes. Again, nothing is said. I sit there for a time. I've finished, and Sophie still has her eyes closed. 'I think we should shower. Ready?' I ask Sophie.

'Fuck… Just give me a minute. That was the strangest sensation, the most amazing… Weird. Kinky. A feeling that is so hard to describe but feels fucking amazing. Yet, so… intimate.' Sophie whispers the last word.

'Shower.' I lean in and kiss her.

CHAPTER FOURTEEN

Annie

Sophie and I make our way into the shower. We stand under the cascading water, holding each other. There is something to be said for being naked and feeling the softness of a woman's body against yours. Feeling their curves, skin on skin. Soft skin and hard erect nipples.

My fingers are trail up and down Sophie's back, as her nails scrape down my own, leaving tingles and shivers in their wake. My breath quickens, and my heart beats faster. Sophie kisses me hard.

Stepping back, she turns the shower on with one hand, her other hand never leaving mine. Whispering in my ear, 'Now, this is my dance and I'm leading. I will be washing you, then we will see how many times I can make you come using this,' as her fingers slide across my clit, 'and this.' Sophie brings her tongue to my mouth and kisses me with sweetness.

She leans into my ear, 'My tongue won't be so gentle next time, not where it's going.' My God! What this woman does to me. What she is going to do to me.

I could kiss her for forever, but I can tell she has other plans.

'Turn around,' Sophie says.

I turn, giving Sophie one more side glance before she is out of my line of vision. My back to her, her hand reaches in front of me picking up the sponge and lathering it in shower gel. Tantalising, Sophie starts at my shoulders, washing her way down my back. Not missing a spot. Now and then she plants small kisses down my spine.

Sophie is in no hurry and I am in heaven, enjoying the feeling's she's awakening. Eventually, she makes her way down to my butt and washes each cheek. She places the sponge on the shelf and puts some gel on her hands. One of Sophie's hands slides between my butt cheeks. Whoa! What the heck is she doing! *Just go with it, Annie. Just go with it!*

Sophie is washing my arse and her fingers are massaging my anus. I close my eyes, taking in the most different of sensations. Who thought I would ever enjoy this? No one has ever done this before. I grind my arse back into Sophie's hand for more contact. Just as I was getting into it, her hand slides forward and Sophie is washing my pubic area from behind. My eyes still closed, I relish everything she's doing to me. Again, just as I'm getting into it, Sophie pulls away. She is being such a tease, a good tease too.

Sophie whispers in my ear, 'Can't neglect the rest of your body, I promised to wash all of you.'

Sophie picks up the sponge and encourages me to turn around to face her and starts washing my arms. My fingers. Sophie rinses my fingers and with slow, painful intent, inserts one of my fingers into her mouth, her eyes never leaving mine. I feel like I'm about to come right then. She then turns me around again so my back is to her.

Sophie is standing so close to me that I can feel her nipples rubbing against my back. She picks up the sponge and proceeds to wash, no, massage my breasts. My nipples. So gently. *Fuck.* We both moan and I turn to kiss her. We kiss hard, like we can't get enough of each other.

Her hand is on my nipple, rolling it between her fingers, her other hand sliding down my stomach to massage my clit. She is driving me crazy with desire. We kiss as she pushes me against the wall, gliding two fingers into me, pumping into me. I move in sync with Sophie's actions. *Ohhh… fuck.* She keeps pumping, and her other hand grabs my hand and puts it on my clit. In a whisper she says, 'I want you to come. Show me how you come.'

Obediently, I rub my clit in small circles. I am so close and Sophie can feel it. Taking a slow step back, she watches me masturbate. Her eyes meet mine just as I come. I shake. My legs feel like they won't hold me and we lock eyes, not breaking eye contact. I lean my head back to rest on the wall, trying to get my breathing under control. Sophie removes her fingers; I place my hand over hers. 'Not yet, leave them where they are.'

After a few minutes I grab her hand and remove her fingers, moaning at the loss of contact; her eyes are glassy. Taking Sophie's hand, I clean every finger. My hand goes behind her head and I pull her into a tender kiss.

CHAPTER FIFTEEN

Annie

We make our way out of the shower, our skin flushed and slightly wrinkled for being in the water a little too long. I grab a towel off the shelf to hand to her. As I turn to grab another, I feel Sophie drying my back. 'You'll get cold,' I say.

Sophie ignores my comment and continues to dry me. She has taken complete control and wants to do this her way, so I let her. She dries me. Everywhere. She looks up at me occasionally, but overall Sophie is focused on doing the job well. Kneeling down, drying between my legs, down to each and every toe. How safe, how secure, she makes me feel. She wraps the towel around me, then dries herself.

Sophie takes my hand, leading me back to the bedroom and tells me in a soft voice. 'I want you laying in the middle of the bed.' I do as I'm told. Standing in front of me, bit by bit she opens her towel, letting it drop to the floor.

'You are perfect,' I say, taking her all in. 'You. Are. Beautiful,' I say, looking straight into her beautiful, sparkling blue eyes.

Sophie crawls up the bed on hands and knees. 'Open your legs.'

Sophie takes her weight through her hands, hovering over me. She takes a nipple into her mouth, then moves over and matches what she did to the other nipple. Sucking. Biting. Tasting. Making her way up to my neck; kissing, sucking, leaving little marks along the way, smirking as she does; teasing me, knowing very well this is driving me crazy. Sophie moves her lips to mine, hovering for a second. Then slowly, her lips meet mine. It's the softest of kisses, but we can both feel the passion rising again. Tongues dancing around one another; neither one wanting to dominate.

Leaving my lips, Sophie tells me to expose my clit. I am under her spell. I do as I'm told, not sure, not knowing what's coming next. She grinds her pubic bone over my clit. With slow regular movements and just enough pressure, she grinds into me and I match her rhythm as Sophie moves down then grinds upward, never losing the connection. With the pressure getting firmer, our pace and breath quickens. Sweat builds up; all the time Sophie is looking into my eyes. Faster still. Never losing rhythm. I groan as I feel my orgasm building. I love this sensation, the long slow build up. Sophie never loses the pace, never loses pressure, never loses the connection between us.

'Oh, my fuck… oh… fuuuck.'

Sophie is using her pubic bone to put pressure on my clit. Riding it. My nipples haven't been kissed, no ministrations on any other part of my body. Only the feeling of her pubic bone over my clit. Her hands are on either side of me taking her own weight. I can't hold out any longer. It's there. It's close. I can feel it. I close my eyes, building, climbing. And then… I come with an almighty moan, my whole body going into spasm.

What a release. Bliss. Pure bliss. My breathing is ragged as

I lie there, my eyes closed, savouring the sensations that make my entire body tingle. Sophie kisses me ever so gently, and whispers in my ear, 'I haven't finished yet. I want to fuck you with my tongue. Now!'

Sophie kisses me again, hard. I feel her passion transferred in that kiss. 'Can I taste you? Can I fuck you? With my tongue? I want to,' Sophie says, her voice husky and full of desire.

CHAPTER SIXTEEN

Annie

My breathing is still ragged, but how can I refuse Sophie? Even the way she talks, makes my clit twitch. I want Sophie to taste me; for her to make me come again but I am too sensitive. Sophie is relentless, insatiable; hunger in her eyes. Sophie won't be happy till satisfied and her craving fulfilled by making me come again with her tongue.

With deliberate movements, she makes her way down my belly, kissing me as she goes. Sophie takes a deep breath. She too, now addicted to the sweet smell of an aroused woman. She places her tongue on my red, swollen orb, knowing I am sensitive from the previous orgasm. Her tongue moves in light circular motions; the feeling is sublime, and she knows just the right amount of pressure that makes me want to come. I don't want to… I want to saviour, taste, feel… everything. Those small circles Sophie is doing over my rigid clitoris… *Ohhh. My. God.*

She feels me building and pulls back, gliding her mouth to lap up my juice. Bit by bit, she traces her tongue back up to my clit; sucking on it with light teasing nips.

'Fuuuuck!' I yell. The sensations are driving me crazy.

Sucking. Biting. Licking. It's like she, or I, can't get enough. Just when I thought I wanted gentle; Sophie knew better. Like a woman possessed, she is about to throw me over the edge. Sucking. Nipping. Licking. I can feel my orgasm mounting. Then at the perfect moment, Sophie's hand comes up; I am oblivious, until she pulls on my nipple.

'Oh, my fucking God!' I explode and it's the biggest, most intense, orgasm I can ever remember, lasting longer than normal. I see stars. I am floating. Sophie stills her tongue as it remains on my clit and she moans into me.

'You have utterly exhausted me,' I gasp, breathless from Sophie's ministrations. Sophie senses my trying to catch my breath as my orgasm rides out, and starts to use her skilled tongue again.

'No… No… I'm too… Ohhh fuuck…' This orgasm arrives quicker. Although short, it is intense. After a while, I open my eyes, not knowing if I fell asleep or blacked out. Sophie is there, smiling, her arm draped over my stomach, her leg across mine. The smile on her face is infectious; I don't think her grin can get any bigger.

'I made you come. I made a woman come. I never thought it would feel so good,' Sophie says, still smiling. 'I made you come.'

'Darling, you made me come four times. No woman has ever done that so fast.'

Sophie's grin is still there. She is on a high. I kiss her, tasting myself on her lips. We both moan into a soft kiss, immersed in total and utter exhaustion.

'I cannot believe you have never slept with a woman,' I say. 'You… are… absolutely… amazing.'

We cuddle. About to doze off, the last thing I hear Sophie

say is, 'I made a woman orgasm. Wow...'

I kiss the top of her head. Sophie has nodded off to sleep with her sweet smile planted on her sweet lips.

Sophie

I don't know where that came from. I'm surprised and a little in shock with myself. When I walked into Annie's I had no intention of doing that. She makes me feel alive, indestructible. Able to do anything. Even so, I'm quite surprised that it came easy to me. I was very turned on when hearing her come that I almost had an orgasm myself. It's such a powerful aphrodisiac.

I feel like I could walk on air. Nothing has ever felt so good. This was new to me, a fantasy of sorts. I made a woman come; but more importantly, I made *Annie* come. Now I understand when Annie says she could never get enough of me because I don't think I'll ever get enough of her.

Thank goodness for the internet. I made sure I deleted my searches before I switched off the computer. Imagine the kids turning on the computer and discovering what I was looking for. *Mum, why were you researching how to make love to women?* I'd be horrified; maybe they would think it was their father. Either way I do not want my children exposed to it.

When I'm with Annie, it feels like nothing is off limits, like everything is so natural. To wash her like I did, something so simple, so personal, I have never felt so close to a lover before. I don't think Annie is used to someone taking control. It took a while for her to let me do what I have been fantasising about since first I laid eyes on her at the gallery.

CHAPTER SEVENTEEN

Annie

We wake sometime later, still in the same position wrapped around each other. I kiss the top of her head, and her eyes flutter open, then close. 'You are so cute,' I say laughing.

Sophie opens one eye and looks up at me. 'And what are you laughing at?'

'You when you're trying to wake up,' I say and kiss the tip of her nose. She leans on to her back and stretches; a big, long stretch. 'Well, I can see you liked that,' I add.

Sophie looks down at her nipples and laughs. 'You are such a perv!' She pulls the sheet up and smiles, 'It's cold in here, that's all. Okay?'

'Whatever you think, but the heating's on.' Sophie blushes when I say this.

'I still think you're a perv,' Sophie says in her husky, sexy as fuck voice.

'Yeah, but I only perv over you,' I say and lean in to kiss my beautiful girl.

'Well, that's okay then. Don't let me see you eyeing any other girls,' Sophie says, feigning sternness.

'It's only you.'

'Then that's okay,' Sophie purrs as she reaches up and kisses me.

'Keep that up and we'll never leave… Come on let's shower, we smell of sex. I want to take you out for dinner,' I say in a jovial, light tone.

Sophie freezes, her eyes wide. 'What's wrong?' I ask.

'You mean 'out' out?' Sophie asks.

'Yeah, I thought we could go out for dinner. I haven't eaten today,' I say with some trepidation.

Sophie and I both lie there in silence for a few minutes. Neither of us uttering a word. We're both lying on our backs on the bed not touching, feeling like an eternity in the silence.

I ask the question, not sure if I want to hear the answer. 'You don't want to be seen out with me? Is that it?' Sophie senses my hurt. Women can be quite perceptive at reading each other. Is it a woman thing? Two women together. Do a man and a woman together have it? I don't know. It's only been women for me and I pick up on it.

'No, no, no,' Sophie says as she rolls and straddles me, grabbing both my hands and holding them in hers. 'No, that's not it at all.' Sophie adds, 'What if I run into someone I know? What if someone sees us?'

I smile as I understand her fear. 'If we go out for dinner, we'll probably run into a lot of people. This is London and we're just two friends out for dinner. No one will ever guess that we've been in bed all afternoon having mad passionate sex.' I smile, hoping it will put Sophie at ease.

'I can put on the heels, don the dress, hair done, make-up on. I've been told I can pull off the lipstick lesbian look quite well.

No one will ever think I'm a lesbian.' I wink at Sophie. 'Come on, shower.'

Sophie smiles and we get up, walking hand in hand into the shower.

'Ready?' I ask.

'Sure, just two friends out for dinner,' Sophie says, a little apprehension in her voice.

Sophie

Why am I so anxious about going out for dinner with Annie? I don't have it tattooed on my forehead that I'm having the best sex in my entire life. What would be wrong if I ran into someone I know? Although, how would I introduce Annie? '*May I introduce my friend Annie. She is THE most amazing and attentive lover I have ever had. Affair? No of course I'm not having an affair.*' But I am. I *am* having an affair.

There is no other word for it. How would I feel if I found out Hugo was having another affair? It was years ago, and I'd been devastated at the time. But would it bother me now? I should have left him then. The children were a lot younger. But I can't do that to them now. I couldn't have done it then. Now they have their GSE's and A levels coming up, and that's an important part of their schooling. Doesn't get much bigger. I need to stay a while longer. I try to push my anxieties out of my head. 'Yeah, two friends out for dinner,' I say, trying to hide my anxiety.

Annie

'We can stay in if you're unsure of this,' I suggest, trying to keep the hurt out of my voice.

'No, it's fine. Maybe I'm just a little paranoid.'

'Come on then. You look absolutely beautiful by the way.' I give Sophie a long lingering kiss, before we jump into a cab. Our conversation is light in the cab and we sit with a little distance between us.

'Where you off to ladies?' the cabbie asks.

'Can you drop us near Soho, thanks.' I know there are lots of nice restaurants to choose from. London cabbies have the gift of the gab and we have a few laughs as he tells us about some of the restaurants he would recommend.

Sophie relaxes and I squeeze her hand. Sophie smiles back at me.

'Have a good night, ladies,' the cabbie says, with a wink, when we arrive at our destination.

'I'm sure we will, thank you,' I answer.

'Laters,' the cheery cabbie says before driving away.

'What is it with that bloody saying,' I mumble.

Sophie and I wander down the little streets of Soho. Making small talk about places we've been, films we've seen, books we've read. Conversation flows, never feeling awkward. We pause at a few restaurants and peruse the menus displayed in the front windows. 'I like the look of this one,' we say in unison. The restaurant is Edwardian in design. High ceilings with large windows that look out onto cobblestone streets. It's a French inspired menu and we both are lovers of cheese; how could we go past this one? It looks warm and inviting, the diners all chatting and animated.

Sophie adds, 'There are things on here that really appeal to me. What about you? Anything take your fancy?'

I grin at Sophie. 'A lot takes my fancy, but the food looks good too. This one it is then,' I say. We wait to be seated, standing a little in from the large doorway. 'Table for two please,' I say when the waitress comes over.

'Window seat?' the waitress asks, pointing to the table right by the window.

'No thank you,' I say, glancing at Sophie who looks a little pale at the idea of such a visible seat. I try not to let it bother me. 'Do you mind if we take the table in the corner?'

'Certainly. This way please.'

I usher Sophie ahead, hoping she takes my lead. Sophie takes the seat facing the door, as I hoped she would. I figure she can keep an eye on people arriving, in case she sees someone she may know. Sophie smiles, realising what I was doing. 'Thank you.'

I smile back at Sophie and we order, not realising how ravenous we both are.

We slip into easy conversation again, pausing now and again to eat.

'You are so comfortable with yourself,' Sophie says. 'With your sexuality, has it always been like that for you?'

'Yes, pretty much. I've never hidden myself away. You either accept me as I am or you don't, I'm not bothered. I am what I am, as the song goes.'

'How did your parents handle it when you came out?'

Silence engulfs us. I try to gather my thoughts, but eventually reply. 'They kicked me out.'

CHAPTER EIGHTEEN

Annie

'What happened? Did they really kick you out? Literally made you leave?' Sophie says in a whisper.

'Yes, they did. People I knew, friends, would always tell me I was gay or at least bisexual. I would often tell myself and others that I slept with guys so I couldn't be gay. I had lesbian friends who would take me to the only gay pub in my hometown. I would just hang with them and their friends, have a few beers, a laugh, a night out, then go out with my straight friends and have the same great night. A few drinks, a laugh, a dance.

'When I look back, and think about it, I've come to the conclusion that I slept with men to try and say to myself: see I'm straight, I sleep with men. But in the back of my mind I knew I was gay. I just wasn't ready to face it or admit it. I've never been in a real relationship with any man. It was always very casual.

'I was at a Christmas party. 18th December 1990. Yes, I still remember the date.' I smirk at Sophie. 'It was an important day for me.'

18th December 1990

Outside, leaning in a doorway, I draw in a breath of fresh air. My head feels a little clouded from the few drinks I'd had. There are people milling about, chatting. That's when I see Jenny approaching me. We talk for a little about the party, each other. Turns out she's a friend of a friend. I watch her mouth as she talks and an urge to kiss her overtakes me. Perhaps it is the alcohol, but I feel a little braver than normal. I lean in, my lips connecting with hers. "Merry Christmas!" I say as I pull away, feeling it was the most natural thing in the world yet never having kissed a woman before.

We kiss again, long and slow. My hands go under her shirt and to her breasts. My god! Nothing had ever felt so good. Everything became clear. A weight lifted from my shoulders; I felt it free me. This is what I want, this is me, this is it; this has been missing.

I am… I am a lesbian. It's the most amazing feeling in the world. I've had a few drinks but I *know*. My world changed. I felt alive; free.

*

Coming back to the present, I clear my throat having just recounted the encounter to Sophie. 'I had found the real me. We dated for a month, and during that month my parents went overseas for two weeks. While they were away my sisters discovered what was happening, and who I was dating, or rather the sex of whom I was dating, and they were not impressed.

'My parents came back from their holiday; we were having our usual family Sunday night dinner with my married sisters and my parents. I was my usual self, but my sisters refused to speak to me. I gave up and met up with Jenny. We decided to go up to the beach for some quiet time. We'd just got to the beach and noticed two men fishing. Jenny's father and brother! I should have taken that as an omen. I returned home later that night to find my parents sitting on the lounge and a look of thunder on their faces. I walked into, "We want to talk to you." And I thought, *I bet you do.* My mother's first words were. "Are you having a lesbian relationship with this woman?"

'I thought to myself, *I wouldn't be having a lesbian relationship with a man now, would I?* But I realised it wasn't the time for sass. She'd spat it out with such venom, but I ignored her tone and without hesitation I said it was true. I didn't want to lie. I couldn't lie. "This is who I am, this is me."'

A tear escaped down my cheek and Sophie leaned across the table and wiped it away with her thumb.

I continued, 'Then the tirade started from them both. My father who always let my mother deal with family matters didn't sit back this time. I had both of them spitting at me. "You're sick. You're disgusting. It's not natural. You're not normal. You need to see a psychiatrist."

'This went on for a good twenty minutes. For once I just sat there because I knew I couldn't change, there was no going back. As much as this hurt them, it would hurt me more if I lived my life as a lie. I listened to their rage in silence and their final words were, "You either go straight or move out of home." I replied, "Is that it? Have you finished?" They both answered yes in unison. So, I told them, "I'll move out because I can't change who I am. This is me."

'No words were spoken between my parents from that point

on. I moved out a week later. I can still remember that final walk out of my family home, the only home I had ever known. My life had changed but I also knew it was going to change more and there was no going back. I hoped it would get better between all of us. As I put the last of my possessions in my car, I walked back into my house. My mother was standing at the kitchen sink, staring out the window with silent tears down her cheeks and me, behind her, shedding the same silent tears. I put my house key on the kitchen bench and got in my car to begin a new chapter in my life.'

I look up at Sophie, not realising that for the last ten minutes, as I recounted my story I had been staring at the table, my eyes prickling with tears. Her arms rest on the table, tears rolling down her cheeks. I rub her forearm. It's the most innocent spot I can touch.

'Please don't cry,' I say. She reaches over with her other hand and takes my hand in hers. It feels so nice. Comforting.

'Did you ever see your parents again?'

I smile. 'Yes, I did. Eventually.'

CHAPTER NINETEEN

Annie

January 1991

'A month has gone by since I left my parents' house. My great-aunt, bless her, invites Jenny and I up to her home every week.

'She tells me how the family are and what has been happening, how she'd tried to talk to Mum. But Mum being Mum won't listen. Stubborn. Every week when Aunty sees Mum, she tells her she saw me. She listened but then would talk about something else. She knew I was okay, at least she didn't say, "I don't want to hear about her."

'About a month after I moved out, my younger sister came around to the house Jenny and I had moved into to tell me about a family gathering. Mum wanted to know if I would be there. "Of course, I will be there!" I almost knocked her over with my over-enthusiastic answer. I think it was hard for my sister to come around and ask me to come along. Not that Marnie didn't want me to, I think she was nervous that I was going to lose my temper with her, it wasn't her fault, she was just a kid.

'Marnie's cheeks were flushed as she said, "It's just an

invitation for you, sorry." I could feel her anxiety.

"'It's okay," I said as I smiled at her. "See you Sunday, I'm looking forward to it."

'Sunday came and the family gathered. It was a tad awkward at first. It was great to see my nieces and nephews. I spent most of the afternoon playing with them, that was easier all round. It felt like no one could talk to me anymore – that I was no longer the same person – yet it was still the same me. My sexuality hadn't changed me, it made me the true me.

'Later in the evening Mum pulled me aside and told me I was always welcome but "that other woman" wasn't. That other woman!

"'The "other woman" has a name. It's Jenny and get used to it because I'm with her, she is my partner." Perhaps I was a bit abrupt, but my mother's words hurt, a lot.

'Talk about a kick in the guts. I didn't want to argue with Mum. I was tired and coming to terms with my sexuality, losing my family at the same time was exhausting. A little contact is better than none. Right?

'We had a few family get-togethers. My sisters and brothers often with their partners, yet I couldn't bring mine. As it turned out, Jenny was having similar issues with her parents. We used to see her parents until they found out she was no longer married to a man. Not that it was a real marriage. Her parents never knew he was gay, and she didn't out him.'

'Jenny was married?' Sophie whispers.

'Marriage of convenience. It worked for them until we met. They were friends for a long time. Jenny wanted the whole white wedding, and his parents were hassling him about getting married and settling down. After a few drinks one night they thought it was a good idea and went through with the whole thing. I think they're still good friends. Anyway, I asked her when we were going to see her parents. I realised we hadn't seen them for about two weeks and she said, "we're not."

'"We're not?" I asked; perplexed. She'd told her parents about me and as she never outed her husband as being gay, it was the same scenario; you're welcome, she's not. I was a homewrecker. Jenny took the stand that if I wasn't invited, she wouldn't be seeing them either. I thought about it and realised I had to take the same course of action. If my parents want to accept me, they have to accept my partner.

'To cut a long story short, my visits became less frequent. Until one day, I had to pick up something from Mum. Jenny came with me but waited outside with our motorbikes. Another thing that irked my mother, we rode motorbikes. I went in and the entire family were there, along with my sweet old Aunt. I greeted everyone, but making small talk was still difficult. Awkward. Sometimes I couldn't wait to get out of there so they could get along with their day, not having to be on tenterhooks because I was around.

'Mum disappeared for a bit, and then I heard the door open. I looked around and my thoughts were… *Holy fucking hell, World War Three is about to break out.* Mum just said, "You all know Jenny."

'Aunty got up and hugged her. "Lovely to see you again dear. And I'll see you both tomorrow?"

'That really broke the ice.

'Mum told me later about her coming around and why she altered her way of thinking. It was the old family doctor who said to her, "Is it the same Annie of yesterday? The same

Annie of a year ago?"

'"Yes," Mum had answered.

'Then he paused, looked at her and said, "If you keep this up, you're going to lose her. Remember you almost lost her once when she was a baby, you want to lose her again? Do you really think Annie has a choice here? That she chose to be a lesbian, and for her to lose the ones she loves? No, I don't think so and deep down neither do you."

'I made peace with my dad before he passed and that was important. But the changes in my mother were astounding. She told everyone I was a lesbian. I asked her one day, "Is there anyone you haven't told?" And her response was, "No one is going to tell me my daughter is gay. I love you and I'm proud of you." What a turn around. Everyone, well almost everyone, came around and accepted Jenny and I,' I explain to Sophie.

'They turned into the most loving and supportive family anyone could wish for. I know it didn't start out great but once they were over, let's say, the surprise, they accepted me and my partner, and future partners as well. I had to give them time. I thank my parents and my siblings for giving me a healthy and positive outlook on being gay, because in the end they were supportive. A lot of my friends when they came out to their families were ostracised. A few don't have contact with their family. One couple I know have been together twenty years, and have no contact with her family. She's tried to reach out to them numerous times, but eventually she gave up. I'm fortunate. I think of the positive outcome and I don't look back.' I say, and I mean every word.

'After the initial bombshell I think most of the family looked back on it and realised I was gay most of my life. My nieces and nephews have grown up with me being a lesbian. To them it's natural to see me with a girl. Now they try and set me up on dates with girls.'

I look across and see a frown cross Sophie's face. 'Stop frowning. I don't go on blind dates anymore. Their intentions are nice though. One sister is still homophobic. She found religion and never accepted homosexuality. I was never invited to her children's parties or any of her family get-togethers. One of her children got married a few years ago. My mother, out of the blue, said to me, "If you're not invited to the wedding I'm not going."

'"What?!" I just screeched to Mum. "You heard," she said.

'"I know I heard it, I just don't believe it. You have to go!" I protested.

'She was so stubborn. She wasn't going to attend if I wasn't invited. I tried explaining that this issue was now my sister's issue. It didn't concern me what they thought of my lifestyle anymore. Still, I pleaded with Mum to go. It was her granddaughter getting married and it would have a bad reflection on both of us. But she wasn't having a bar of it. She thought it was time she stood up to my sister. She drew that imaginary line in the sand and said she should have stood up to my sister and her appalling behaviour long before now. But to make a point over a wedding? Once my mother had made up her mind, that was it; she wasn't going if I didn't get an invitation.'

I look across at Sophie, who is resting her chin on her hand as she gazes at me. 'Sorry, I'm probably talking too much, I'll stop, I've bored you into oblivion, haven't I?'

'No! No! Go on! I love your story. You're not boring me at

all…' I sip my drink before picking up where I left off.

'Like I said, Mum became one of my staunchest supporters. If she was out with friends or acquaintances, and they started speaking about gay people in a derogatory way, Mum would walk away. "Where are you going, Alice, I haven't finished?" some would say.

'"You know I have a gay daughter and while you are putting gays down, male or female, you are putting my daughter down. I won't sit there and listen to any of it," Mum would scold them.

*

Present day

'These days my family are not embarrassed to be seen with me and my girlfriends, they love me without conditions and they just accept me for being me. I love them the same in return. I wasn't sure about one of my brothers, as to how comfortable he was with the whole lesbian thing. I thought he could have been a little homophobic too. He never appeared comfortable or relaxed around me. I guess there's no such thing as a *little homophobic,* you either are or aren't. I asked one of my sisters if she thought he was homophobic. She stared at me with a quizzical look and in all seriousness said, "No, he likes leaving the house." I have never laughed so much.'

Sophie and I roar with laughter and notice some of the diners have turned in our direction. We tone down the laughter but keep giggling with tears streaming down our cheeks, unable to stop. 'So, I guess my family, for the most part isn't homophobic.' We giggle some more. 'Mum was my rock. I miss that. I miss my parents,' I say, wiping a tear from my eye.

I'm not sure if it's from the laughter or the emotions telling my story has dredged up. Sophie is still holding my hand.

'See, it all worked out just fine. I got love, respect, and support from my family. What about you? Have you always been attracted to women?' I ask Sophie. She takes a deep breath.

CHAPTER TWENTY

Annie

In a quiet voice, Sophie says, 'I think so. In high school I often had girl crushes; I looked up to female teachers and I just thought it was a stage I was at. Puberty. Hormones… I always had close emotional connections with my female friends, and yet I dated boys. And it was the times. I don't know. I felt it was expected to marry and have children.' She stared into her drink with a grimace.

'Religion I think played a role too; Catholic guilt has lot to answer for! How would my parents have dealt with that? Come home one day, "hey Mum, hey Dad, you know I'm into girls." No. The good daughter doesn't do that. It would not have come as a surprise if, Connie, my rebellious sister, had said it. But me? The eldest and feeling as though I was responsible for everyone, even my Granny who lived with us, no way. The family ran a shop and I would always look after my younger siblings while my parents worked. With the long hours, I guess I had to shoulder some responsibility and take some of the burden off them.

'My father would get up early and go to the markets before

opening the shop. He would come in late in the evening and be exhausted; Mum or Granny would make him a tea and he'd go upstairs. Most nights we were asleep by the time he got home. Having only sisters, with Mum and Granny at home, I was used to a home full of women. Even our dogs were female. I come from a long line of strong women, somehow, I feel I have let them down.' Sophie says, despondent as she gazes off into the distance. She returns her gaze to me and continues, 'Sorry, I don't know what made me tell you that. I guess thinking back to the time I started to have feelings for women. I had been going out with my husband a few years and it was just a natural progression. People expected me to marry him, which wasn't a bad thing. I've got two great kids and would lay down my own life for them. My parents liked him; he liked my parents. But…' I sense she is trying to find the words. I wait patiently, there's no need to rush her.

'I always felt something was missing – that I wasn't complete,' she says. 'I got caught up with the marriage, a husband, a career, the children, and feeling like I couldn't disappoint my parents. My needs were swept aside. My kids needed a loving home, somewhere they would be safe. I was happy, please don't think I wasn't. But now the kids are older and I can't deny these feelings any longer. And not women, one woman.

'The first woman I fell in love with was my music teacher. She was stunning and nurturing of my talent. She made me fall in love with music and took the time to listen to me. After school, aside from some friends, I missed her the most. It was like I broke up with her because I knew I'd never see her again.

'I often wonder how people cope in prison, but I can justify my lack of care in that because they broke the law and they deserve to be there. But… I feel like I'm in a prison of my own making. I'm cheating on my husband and guilty of that but worse, I'm not living my true existence; I'm conforming. I'm just… I'm just not ready to come out yet, and that makes me feel like a coward. It's not about my kids; it's not about my less than perfect marriage. It's about me. But I can't deny this attraction. I want to explore all of this desire and let it evolve for us.'

Sophie continues, wanting to get the feeling into the open. 'When the two of us are together it's like the rest of the world doesn't exist. It's where I belong, in your arms and I feel safe. It feels… like home. Like you said before, the most natural thing in the world, the pieces have finally fallen into place. And now, what do I do?' Sophie says, tears welling in her eyes

I look into Sophie's eyes. I see her tears and feel her fear. 'Baby steps, one at a time.'

'You never pressure me. You never tell me what I'm doing is wrong.'

I smirk at the comment and a blush tints her cheeks. Sophie tilts her head and smiles. I haven't seen her beautiful smile light her face since she started sharing her story and I'm relieved to see the sparkle back in her blue eyes.

'It's not fair to you. I sleep with you and then go back home and try to play happy family and you never get angry. You never question me,' Sophie says her voice cracking.

'What? You want me to get angry with you. Why? You're struggling through this awakening. You don't want me to get angry, you are doing that to yourself. I just want to support you. I knew what I was getting involved in. I walked into this with my eyes wide open. I am so attracted to you and I haven't had this attraction to anyone for so long.'

'What about if I walk away from all this? From you. Where does that leave you?' Sophie whispers.

'If you walk away, I will be hurt. I will miss you. But when I think of you, I will smile at the moments we shared.' I stroke Sophie's fingers. 'I will miss these and what you do with them. I will miss kissing these…' My fingers caress her lips.

Sophie leans over the table and plants the sweetest, gentlest kiss on my lips, then pulls away and whispers, 'I can't walk away.'

'Then don't,' I whisper, my lips ever so close to Sophie's.

We kiss. The kiss deepens as we forget where we are, unhurried and full of our yearning. We pull away as though fighting gravity between us.

'Oops.'

Sophie blushes, and looks around; the restaurant is almost empty and those who are left are in deep conversation. The wait-staff are busy clearing tables and setting them up for the next diners.

'I don't think anyone noticed,' Sophie says.

'Lucky we're in this corner. Tucked away nice and discreet,' I smile. 'Come on, let's go. I think I've put on enough of a show here.' We pay and walk out.

The waitress smiles and holds the door open. 'Thank you, ladies and enjoy your night.'

'Thank you,' we say in unison.

CHAPTER TWENTY-ONE

Sophie

It's so easy to talk to Annie. I've hidden my feelings for women so long I'd forgotten they existed. I had decided on my path, to get married and have children. The attraction I had towards women faded, or perhaps I chose to ignore it, to bury those feelings. I got too busy with life, with my children. I forgot about me, and if I want to be honest, I am attracted to women. But the thought of admitting it openly petrifies me. I don't need to come out. What is this Annie and I share? There is no talk of me coming out, it's not something we have talked about. I'm a married woman who has fallen in love with a woman.

What if what happened to Annie by her family happens to me? Her family accepted her, and they didn't take too long in the great scheme of time, but things are different for me. Annie didn't have kids or a husband at stake. I could lose everything. My children. My family. Would I get sacked if my work found out? No, that would never happen, I've seen the policies. But would it change the relationship I have with my colleagues? I've never heard anyone speak ill of the LGBT group at the university. Would Hugo take the children away from me?

On the other hand, meeting Annie has ignited this flame. With Annie I don't have to pretend. I feel like the Sophie I was meant to be. Yet the thought of saying it out loud, telling friends, petrifies me. How will they react? Will I lose my friends? And what about Emily and Adrian? Would my children want to be seen with their mother and her girlfriend in public? I can't do that to them, not just yet. They'll get teased and bullied. I can't do that. Let's just have fun, Annie and I. We're not hurting anyone. We're not hurting each other. *Who am I kidding? This can only end in disaster.*

CHAPTER TWENTY-TWO

Annie

Wandering along the streets of London it appears to be everyone is out. We blend into the crowd, chatting as we walk. Will we ever tire of talking? Our conversations can become heated, debating issues and solutions to world problems. We have differing opinions and we listen to each other's point of view. We laugh at it even if we clash.

Sophie stops but I don't notice and continuing to walk and talk to myself. After a few paces I stop, looking over my shoulder to see Sophie standing in the street with a grin on her face.

'Thanks for letting me make a goose of myself as I talked to no one. I was wondering why people were looking at me strangely and worse, taking a wide berth!' I laugh, walking back to Sophie, who gives a throaty chuckle.

'I did notice the people looking at you.' Sophie has a good laugh. The sound is sweet and it makes me smile.

'Why have you stopped?'

'I want to go in.' Sophie lets her eyes dart to a sign above us, one for the lesbian nightclub we are in front of. 'I want to dance with you where no one cares that two women are dancing together. Just you and me.'

'Are you sure?'

'Let's just go in before I lose my nerve…'

We walk in and as soon as we're off the street and through the doors, Sophie grabs my hand. I look down at our entwined fingers. 'I like this. It feels good.'

'It does. It feels right… Can I kiss you?' Sophie asks.

I laugh. 'Bit late for that isn't it?' We kiss, and I feel Sophie relax into my arms, melting into me. 'You feel great in my arms. Let's go downstairs, it's a bit quieter down there.'

Sophie eyes me with humour. 'So, you've been here before?'

'Once or twice.' I grin. 'Well, I am a single girl living in London, who likes to dance.'

'Are you single now?' Sophie asks.

'I can say I am very happy seeing the person I am admiring right at this very minute. And I could admire her for a very, long, time,' I say looking into Sophie's eyes.

Sophie grabs my face with both hands and lunges to my lips with a feverish heat. Her wet lips engulf mine and her tongue lashes into my waiting mouth. She kisses me like she has never kissed me before. Deep. Passionate. With so much lust. She stops, desperate for a breath and throws her head back as her tongue dances over her lips.

'Let's get a drink,' she says, taking hold of my hand and we walk to the bar. 'Just staking my claim. Let them know you're with me.' Sophie grins as she radiates pride like a hunter after a kill.

'It's me that should be careful of you, I've seen the girls looking at you, admiring you. They've never seen you before so they're curious. I think the phrase used is fresh meat. New blood is another disgusting term. When they see someone new, they get excited, like cats on heat, hence why I don't go out that often,' I explain. 'I've been here maybe three or four times and that's when Alessandra flies in from Zurich. She's one of my best friends. She's deprived of gay girls where she lives so I'm helping a friend.' I wink at Sophie.

'You're a good friend.' Sophie acknowledges with another kiss. 'Thank you.'

The girl behind the bar appears. 'What will it be ladies?' she asks, never taking her eyes off Sophie, who is busy taking in the atmosphere around her and doesn't notice.

I eyeball the barmaid with a *look*. 'My girlfriend and I will have two glasses of champagne please.' I hold eye contact with her as she nods and leaves to get the drinks. She returns a minute later with our drinks in hand and a rather embarrassed look on her face for being caught out. 'How much please?'

'On the house, ladies.'

'Thank you.'

'My pleasure,' she says. 'And sorry about that. I didn't realise she was your girl.'

'No offence taken. Thanks again for the drinks.'

'Champagne,' Sophie says sounding surprised. 'What are we celebrating?'

'Your first dance in a lesbian bar with a gay woman,' I respond as we clink the glasses together.

'How about that dance then?' Sophie asks with that amazing, light-up-the-room smile.

'Would you do me the honour of allowing me to have this dance with you?' I bow, moving to the dance floor where we fit together like we were made for each other.

Sophie whispers in my ear. 'No one even cares we're dancing. Two women dancing together.'

'Welcome to my world baby.' I lean in and kiss her. 'And no one cares we're kissing.' I smile. 'You are so beautiful.'

'I bet you say that to all the girls.'

'No, I don't. Just you,' I say in all seriousness. 'And now show me your moves twinkle toes.'

Some people have moved away from the dance floor leaving a few couples and making it easier to glide around. The song fades and a new tune starts. 'I love this song!' I say. 'This will have to be our song. Come on one more dance.' With that the lyrics start... *You're just too good to be true, can't take my eyes off of you... You'd be like heaven to touch... I wanna hold you so much.*

Sophie and I glide about the dance floor, moving together in beat with the music; Sophie taking my lead. *God. What can't this woman do. She just glides.* The song finishes and we look deep into each other's eyes and kiss with a new passion; a fire erupts in us as our hands caress our bodies and our hunger grinds us together with unbearable longing.

'Take me home,' Sophie moans into my ear as her hips grind against my thigh and our breath quickens. After a minute of savage grinding, I whisper, 'I can't.'

CHAPTER TWENTY-THREE

Annie

Sophie's eyes widen. 'Why not?'

'I just can't.'

'Why? Tell me why. Do you have someone else coming over tonight?' Sophie says, her voice laced with anger.

'It's late and you need to go back home to your husband and children.'

Silence. We just look at each other, words unspoken. I pull Sophie in, and hug her, holding tight.

'I know… I know,' Sophie whispers, 'you're right.'

I take Sophie over to private area of the bar where I can see the tears sparkling in her eyes as the lights in the club flicker over us. One tear rolls down her cheek and I wipe it away with my thumb. I look Sophie in her eyes and say, 'There is nothing I want to do more than take you home, make love to you for all hours, then wake up with you in the morning, in my bed. But… you know you have to go. Don't you think he is going to get a little bit suspicious if you don't come home tonight?' We stand there holding each other tight and I rub Sophie's back. 'It's going to be okay. I promise you; it's going to be alright,' I whisper in her ear.

Sophie turns to look at me and kisses me. She kisses me like it will the last time. Like she can't get enough. I know I have to pull away. I don't want to, but I have to, one of us has to be strong. 'Come on, we should go, you have to get back home.'

'I just need to use the bathroom first.'

'Okay, come on. It's through here.' Sophie walks into a cubicle, and as I walk past, she grabs me by the wrist and pulls me in with her. 'Bloody hell woman!' I laugh. Sophie has a serious look on her face.

'Please.' She grabs my hand. 'Please, I can't go home like this.'

'Oh fuck,' I moan. Sophie puts my hand in her panties. 'Jeezus… Fuck,' I whisper, 'you're so wet. So, fucking wet.'

'Just fuck me. Make me come.' Sophie begs, pleading with me.

Three of my fingers glide into her wetness and I sense she doesn't want this desire to be gentle, so I pump my fingers in – out – in – out. She is so tight that my three fingers are curled over each other into a long probe that slides in and out of her with rhythmic ease.

'Ohhhh, you feel so good.' I keep pumping as she is close to orgasm. I slip my hand out and find her rigid clit.

'Harder, fucking harder.' Sophie cries out through clenched teeth. She moans and I continue rubbing her love button. Sophie's hand is over mine, applying pressure to her pelvis and then in one long moan, she comes in a wave of trembling muscle spasms and gasping breaths which make my own juices flow between my legs. I put my hand over her mouth to stifle her sounds as the bathroom door opens.

Sophie's eyes are closed as she rides out her orgasm, still with my hand over her mouth and in one quick movement, Sophie nips at my hand. It surprises me and I yelp.

'You alright in there?' a girl asks on the other side of the cubicle.

'Yep, just knocked my hand, thanks for asking,' I say as I glare at Sophie. Well, I try to glare but end up smiling. Sophie mouths "sorry" with such a sexy smile and I mouth "payback" to her. We listen for the others to leave and make our way out. We're at the sink washing our hands, looking at each other in the mirror. 'You know you are bad. Very… very bad.'

Sophie smiles in a way I love and her eyes radiate also.

'Come on, let's get out of here,' I say, grabbing her hand.

I brush Sophie's cheek with my fingers. 'You know we can't spend the night together. You have to go and it's late already. I want you, believe me I do. But…'

'I know. I know. I have to go home sometime,' Sophie says her voice full of dejection and her eyes full of sadness. Putting Sophie in a cab, with one last kiss on her soft cheek, we say our farewells. I watch it drive away with Sophie as I sigh and seek my own cab home.

Sophie

Sitting in the cab I'm a mess of conflicting emotions. On the one hand I'm floating on air because I've never, ever, done anything like I just did with Annie, dragging her into the cubicle and making her finger-fuck me. I cannot get enough of her. I couldn't go home the way I was feeling. I needed that release and that in itself is foreign to me, before now I've always been in control of my emotions and Hugo has never gotten me into that sort of mess. Maybe back in the day, the early days, but I can't remember it ever being like this with Hugo. We just got into a comfortable friendship from the beginning of our relationship and we have been friends before we started going out in school. At university, we were part of a wider group. After about a year, we slept together; *a drunken shag* as he called it. We kept going with it though as we were young and neither of us seeing anyone else. That's how our marriage happened; it was just the next step in the comfortable flow we had created.

How am I going to explain to Hugo why I was out so late? Let alone who I was out with. I check my phone and there is nothing from him. He mustn't be too concerned. I'd dropped the kids at their friends and I know the parents as they often have sleepovers, either at their place or ours. As families, we've had holidays together and been friends for many years, so I know Emily and Adrian are in safe hands. Maybe Hugo's gone to the pub, oblivious to the time then it would be possible he has fallen asleep on the lounge.

Opening the front door, I hear the television on. Finding Hugo where I'd predicted (and hoped), I sneak upstairs and change into my pyjamas. Coming back down with a blanket, I place it over Hugo; knowing if he is warm enough, he'll sleep till morning, thus avoiding his questions and having to lie. Again. *Is my life becoming one big lie?*

In bed I can't sleep. I lie awake staring at the ceiling and thinking. I'm betraying Hugo. This isn't his fault. He didn't push me into the arms of another woman.

*

In the morning, I'm woken by light knocking on the door as Hugo enters with a poor attempt at being quiet. 'I didn't want to disturb you in case you were still sleeping,' he mumbles in a bland apology. 'I've made you a cuppa and you did have the last biscuit, until I dropped it on the floor… well, then George snuffled it up. Got to be quick around that dog. Sorry about that.' Hugo places the cup of tea on my bedside table. 'I'm going to get some things from the supermarket. I'm making more biscuits this afternoon. I'll pick up the kids on the way home. Do you need anything?' he asks.

'No thank you, I'm fine. Just check if we have enough cereal for the kids.' He gets a sweater from the wardrobe, making small talk about his afternoon the day before and I feel a tingle of concern. What if he asks what I got up to? But then he comes over and kisses me on the cheek and walks out after saying goodbye. I hear the car start and pull out of the drive and then I burst into tears. I sob and can't stop.

What am I doing to my marriage, to my family? He's not a bad man. I'm just not in love with him anymore and that breaks my heart. Will I break Hugo's heart? I need to stop being a coward and just be honest with everyone. The tears won't stop flowing. I don't know where to start.

CHAPTER TWENTY-FOUR

Annie

Weeks drift by with long hours and our intimate texts and phone calls to each other. I never tire of listening to Sophie's melodic voice. Her stories make me laugh and she has the kind of laugh that is infectious to all who fall in its distance.

We arranged to meet up on Friday afternoon. Sophie can get away early from the university as she has been putting in longer than normal days in the weeks leading up to midterm break. Now, she can relax a bit and wind down and we can spend time together. The separation has been trying and as much as we talk on the telephone, it doesn't come close to holding each other. There's comfort that comes from sitting and talking and laughing in person.

Sophie arrives at my house at the same time as I arrive home after picking up groceries on the way from work. We've had a busy week and opted for an easy dinner at my place. Cooking relaxes me and tonight, we both wanted something simple that could pair with a little red wine, of course. I've decided on an easy-to-cook pasta dish. Food, wine, and an evening with Sophie. Nothing could feel more perfect.

I wait for her to get out of the car. She doesn't see me at first then, like she can feel my eyes on her, she stops and smiles. That beautiful smile I was first taken with at the gallery; a smile that can melt an iceberg and illuminate a room. Both of us just stand there for a long moment, admiring one another.

'Come on you, don't stand out there all night, I've got a warm house waiting for us,' I say breaking us out of our trance.

Sophie gives a husky throaty laugh. 'I'm coming! I'm coming! Hold on to your britches.'

'Britches? What century are you living in?' I laugh as she shuts her car door.

'Oh, hush, don't be curt,' she snaps playfully.

'It just gets better, I don't think I've ever heard the words hush and curt used, let alone in the same sentence together.' I laugh as Sophie walks closer to me and I lean in to give her a kiss on the cheek. 'You just get more adorable every time I see you.'

'I can live with that. Now get me inside please. It's freezing out here.'

Opening the door, I step aside to allow Sophie inside. We take off out coats and hats, putting them on the hat rack as we chat away about the day and the weeks we have been apart. As I listen to her talking, she's busying herself by putting things away. She is immaculately dressed. She stops, notices me looking at her. 'What? Why are you looking at me like that, and stop smiling, I'm all embarrassed.'

I take a step towards her and tuck her hair behind her ears, keeping my hands there. 'I've missed you so much. I never realise how much till you're here, in front of me. I love having you here with me. I just love it.'

Sophie leans in and kisses me. I feel the warmth of her

tongue entwine with mine as we taste each other's breath in our mouths; feel each other's hold tighten and breath quicken. We break the kiss and stand with our arms around each other. Is there anything this woman doesn't do right? Even just her hug releases the stress from my body.

'I've missed you too. Our schedules don't do our relationship any good.'

'Yep. I guess this is what's being called a grown up and having responsibility. It sucks, Mum,' I say in a whiny voice and we both laugh. 'Do you want to go up and shower or freshen up while I start preparing the food? Thought we'd just have pasta. Is that okay?'

'Perfect. As long as we can curl up on the sofa and cuddle after,' Sophie says with a mischievous glint in her eye as she saunters off to the bathroom.

I'm in so much trouble here. This is only going to end in disaster. But I'm so smitten with her. I can't walk away. I can't let her go. She's perfect in my eyes and perfect for me, but it goes against everything I believe in. Everything I said I would never do again. But I can't help it. She has my heart.

CHAPTER TWENTY-FIVE

Annie

Sophie returns after having a quick shower, and I eye her with suspicion, meandering over to her. 'Those trousers you're wearing look very comfortable,' I wrap my arms around her waist, 'I think they look better on you than they do on me.'

'They will be returned, maybe. I feel close to you when I have your clothes on. Are all girl relationships like this? Sharing each other's clothes, shoes, things like that?'

'Pretty much. Well, the relationships I've had anyway. We just get on and do things, we totally get the whole period thing, we know when things are needed like milk etc. It's just, I don't know, teamwork. I shouldn't judge my lesbian relationships based on straight ones but I have heard women complaining about their husbands, so I can only go on what they say. "He never does the washing, he wouldn't know how to iron a shirt, never remembers we need milk, always asks what's for dinner". We laugh at my imitations. 'Sorry ladies, you're not his mother. You should have nipped that in the bud when you first married him. So, on that note I've prepared the food. I think it's safe to open the wine and pour me a glass. Please,' I ask with a smile and Sophie obliges the job of pouring. 'Cheers. To a nice relaxing evening with great company.' We clink glasses.

We sit on the lounge, music playing in the background, and enjoy our dinner together. The conversation swings around to Jared, and how we met. I explain to Sophie how we first met at the drop-in centre where I was volunteering and how it has progressed over the years.

'After finishing high school Jared did an arts/law degree, finishing with first class honours. He always wanted to study law. He loved the study and was so disciplined; they both were, Daniel and Jared. Daniel was Jared's first and only true love.' I sipped my wine as I spoke. 'Jared loved a good old argument, but he'd always argue with the facts and not in a demeaning way, say if the other person didn't get it. He's just got an amazing mind for retaining information. In high school, he was on the debate team. I went to several of the big debates he was in when he was in college too; he has an amazing mind, very sharp.

'Through university, and even now when time permits, Jared goes back to the drop-in centre and volunteers to hang with the kids and offer support and show them it's not all bad. That they're not the only ones in the world who are gay, like many think they are. He speaks with great regard for the drop-in centre and the positive effect it had on him growing up, and then of his coming out. As soon as the kids see him coming into the centre, they hover around him so he can give each of them a high five, and talk to each one of them so they feel important; he has a great gift for doing that. He talks to them like they are adults and listens to them. He gets excited and animated with them, and it's a natural enthusiasm, not false or put on. When the kids are talking to him, he makes them feel they're the only one in the world, that he has all the time in the world for them, and them alone. Sorry, I digress, I was just thinking, and verbalising.'

'Anyway, Jared met Daniel on his first day on campus. They both enrolled in the same degree, both coming from quiet English towns and wanting to break away. They wanted to discover themselves also and away from where they may be judged for it. They wanted to experience life in a big city, London is perfect for that. Also great to be anonymous, where no one cared or took a second glance at men together. Live and let live, they would often say.'

'They wanted to make a change and a successful life, build a career and find a partner, travel to see the world. They began studying with a few classmates and after a few sessions, they felt the others weren't as serious in their studies, so just the two of them met up and studied. They were focused, and wanted good grades and they liked a little competition; a bit of friendly rivalry. They were proud of each other if one topped the class.'

'It was a great friendship, and what became a beautiful relationship. They had been studying for about six months, getting to know one another. They would spend time with girls from university, going out in a group. Girls would always hit on them and ask them out. One night, Daniel went home with one. He'd had a bit too much to drink and the girl dragged him home. She'd been chasing him for the entire time at uni.'

'Jared didn't see Daniel for a few days after the encounter with… Jillian, I think her name was? Sorry, I remember the strangest things. Anyway, Jared thought he had hooked up with Jillian and left it at that. Jared didn't want to divulge to Daniel that he was gay and by this time, attracted to him. He thought the friendship was too important to lose if he told him he was gay, and that he was attracted to him on many levels, not to mention how gorgeous he thought Daniel was.'

'Daniel came back about four days later and was very quiet; worse, he wouldn't look Jared in the eye. Jared asked him if everything was okay and how Jillian was. She was "fine" was all Daniel said, so Jared didn't push the point. They studied the entire afternoon. Jared felt something had happened in those past four days that he hadn't seen Daniel but knew if Daniel wanted to talk about it, he would, he wasn't going to push him.'

'Jared got up and said he was going for a cup of tea. As he walked past Daniel, he put his hand on his shoulder and asked him if he wanted one, with that, Daniel burst into tears. Jared was taken aback with Daniel breaking down the way he did. Daniel was just sobbing. Jared took him to the couch, and asks, "beer or tea?"

'Daniel looked at Jared with the beautiful blue eyes Jared adored and says, "I think this is a beer story."

'Jared grabbed two beers out of the fridge and handed one to Daniel. Jared sat on the couch opposite as Daniel tried keeping his eyes fixed on the floor in front of him. After about half a beer, Daniel opened up. Jillian had taken him back to her dormitory and she was all over him; told him how much she wanted him. Daniel said he wasn't that drunk but faked it so he could pretend to pass out.'

'He passed out? Why?' Sophie exclaims.

'I assumed that's what young boys and girls got up to while they were at uni. Fresh out of home, discovering themselves, thinking they're the first generation that has discovered sex.'

'It turned out Daniel had always had a crush on Jared. He wasn't sure if he was gay, and his head was spinning with all these emotions he wasn't used to having. He liked Jared but he was a man, and he had never felt anything like this towards another man. He said he was scared to tell him because he may think of him as a freak and he'd tell the whole campus and he would be ridiculed by his friends. He was crying as he was telling Jared. But Jared didn't let him be upset for long.

'He moved over to the couch, sat next to Daniel, his arm around his shoulder as he told Daniel he came out at fifteen and he thought Daniel was the most beautiful person he had ever laid eyes on. He continued to tell him how the first time he laid eyes on him at Freshers Week with the way he dressed and how he moved with nervousness and trying to hide it. I think that's why Jared is a brilliant lawyer, his mind is amazing, remembers the smallest details, every conversation, and he can read people, doesn't miss a beat. I've told him he'll be my memory when I'm old.

'Jared epitomises everything that's good in the world. He has an aura about him and people are like moths to a flame around him. He's funny and charming, he makes everyone feel like they're the only one in the world. He focuses on people, always makes eye contact with them. Both men and women flirt with him, and sometimes go that one step further and ask him out or ask him to go home with them. He just flatters them as he lets them down gently. No one is ever angry with him. He has a gift and he doesn't exploit it. He doesn't make people feel embarrassed when he says he's not interested in dating them at the moment due to other commitments. A moment that has been… let me think,' I ponder for a moment,

'Five years. It was just after Jared's thirtieth birthday but before Daniel celebrated his.'

Sophie is staring at me with eyes wide. 'Five years? Jared hasn't dated for five years? Not anyone? I don't believe it, what you have told me about him, he appears to be a tremendous guy. Daniel must have broken his heart. What did he do? What could be so bad that would stop a great guy dating?' Sophie finished with a hint of bewilderment and anger in her tone.

'Daniel died,' I whisper as I try to hold back tears.

CHAPTER TWENTY-SIX

Annie

'I – I – My God. What happened?' Sophie stutters as her hand raises to her mouth and tears well in her eyes.

'Daniel and Jared were on a night out, celebrating a late birthday for Jared and an early birthday for Daniel. Peter and Simon, who were their lecturers for some subjects at university, went to dinner too. On the walk back to their cars as they crossed a street, the group heard shouting. The noise was coming from down a laneway, and they found a group of five men hitting and kicking two men on the ground. Daniel, without thinking, raced over to try and stop the fighting. He didn't like violence but before Jared could grab him, he was off and in no way thinking of his own safety.'

'He raced towards them yelling, "Guys, come on. Get off them." By the time Jared, Simon and Peter reached the group, Daniel was lying on the ground with blood coming out of his ear and nose. The men had punched him on the side of the head, sending him face first into a brick wall. Jared said it all happened so fast. He cradled Daniel in his arms, apparently saying over and over, "Come on baby wake up, open your eyes baby. Come on, talk to me."

'Simon had already rung for help and the perpetrators had taken off while the other two men were struggling to get up. Peter was trying to calm them; telling them help was on the way. Simon kept checking Daniel to make sure he was still breathing but Simon feared it wasn't going to be a good outcome.'

I stare at nothing, remembering that horrible time.

'That night our lives changed forever,' I continue. 'Simon rang telling me what had happened and where they would be taking Daniel. It was just heart-breaking when I met them at the hospital. I don't think I've ever driven so fast.' Tears flow down my cheeks as the images fill my mind from the night. Sophie's warm hand holds my shaking one and with the thumb of her other hand, she wipes away my tears.

Sophie startles me out of a daydream, as she says, 'What happened after that?'

'Oh, right, yes… Jared told me, from what he could recall, that the ambulance and police didn't take long to arrive and that they put Daniel in a neck brace and inserted a breathing tube. Jared didn't like this and told them Daniel could breathe on his. Pete pulled him aside and told him to focus, that Daniel needed him to be strong and to let the paramedics do their job. It took Pete about ten minutes to make sure Jared calmed down enough to register what Pete was saying. The paramedics stabilised him enough to transfer him to hospital, but said it wasn't possible for Jared to ride in the ambulance, but they could follow. Simon went and got the car and bought it round, but Jared just wouldn't leave Daniel and they had no choice but to let him ride with them in the ambulance.

'At the hospital, they stabilised Daniel enough to prepare him for theatre. There was swelling of his brain and they needed to relieve the pressure. I'd rung Daniel's parents. It was one of the worst calls I've ever had to make. Daniel's mum, Lorraine, was hysterical on the phone. I was hoping that Bob, her husband, would answer the phone as I thought it would be easier to tell him the news. As soon as Lorraine heard my voice, she asked what was wrong, "Are my boys okay?" They were her boys. She loved, and still loves Jared like her own. It devastated everyone,' I say as my voice trails off in a whisper.

'They couldn't put Daniel's surgery off any longer. The staff were amazing. But the surgeon said they held out for as long as possible waiting for Daniel's parents, but they were still a couple of hours away. Daniel went in for surgery. They let Jared and I go up to the operating theatre entrance with him. All the time Jared holding his hand and talking to him, telling him he loved him. Even the nurses from Intensive Care had tears in their eyes by the time we reached the operating theatre. As the doors to the operating theatre closed Jared fell against then slid down the wall and cried the most heart-breaking sound I have ever heard. I just held him. I couldn't say it was going to be alright because I didn't know.

'Twelve years of togetherness. Never any jealousy between them. They partied, did the usual drunken nights while at uni, did drugs once at a nightclub and vowed never ever again. Just a beautiful couple, on the same page with a lot of things. Shared the same values, both champions of the underdog. Sometimes I still can't believe what happened. It was just awful, and so painful, it still hurts.

'Daniel was in the operating theatre for about six hours. His parents had arrived by the time he came out. We couldn't see him till he was back in the intensive care unit. Pete and Simon stayed till they knew Daniel was out of theatre then went home about 4 am. I asked Jared if he wanted me to stay as both their parents were now there and it was family time. He just looked at me lost, and said, "You are family…?" So I stayed.'

CHAPTER TWENTY-SEVEN

Annie

'The neurosurgeon came into the room where we waited, and I'll never forget the look in his eyes; a look of resignation in his eyes. I think with my line of work I get used to reading people. I took a breath to steady myself. He sat down and looked at each of us before telling us Daniel's condition. The initial blow to the head, followed by hitting the wall caused massive bleeding in his brain. Traumatic brain injury, he called it. The bleeding caused the two parts of his brain to move. Midline shift, the Doctor called it. As devastated as we all were some words stuck in my head and even to this day, I hate hearing them. They send shivers over me. The surgeon explained how he had opened Daniel's skull and drained the blood that was causing swelling then found where he was bleeding from and stopped it. The surgeon said the next 48 hours were crucial; the prognosis doesn't look positive due to the mechanism of injury to the brain, he'd said. Which, in my books was a nice way to say Daniel would have brain damage.'

'The surgeon asked if Daniel's parents were the next of kin. They both said at the same time that no, they weren't his next of kin but Jared was his husband and all decisions would come from Jared. Jared spoke up and said, "We will make decisions as a family." The surgeon was honest with us, not that he had been lying but he had been reserved in his explaining of the injury. He said it was one of the worst head injuries he'd seen. He believed the initial punch to the head caused the bleeding, and that he predicted a minimal hope for recovery. He said he hoped he was wrong but twenty years of neurosurgery gave him an excellent indication of what was survivable and what wasn't. And if Daniel did survive, he wouldn't be the same, that the midline shift of his brain was quite significant.'

'We sat in the waiting room in complete silence, not knowing what to say, each one of us trying to grasp the enormity of the situation and come to terms with the condition of Daniel and what had happened. I know I felt like I was in some bad dream. This couldn't be happening; it couldn't be real. Our Daniel, so full of life and protector of the underdog, until it cost him his life. Trying to protect complete strangers because a group of thugs had set upon them. Gutless cowards they were, and these cowards were going to take my friends life. I didn't know these people and yet I hated them.'

I look down at Sophie's hands, still holding mine. 'I should stop,' I say. 'I'm sure you don't want to hear all this.'

'I'd like to know what happened. I'd like to know. Daniel was your friend, and Jared is still a part of your life, please. Tell me the rest,' Sophie whispers, fighting her own tears.

'Okay,' I sigh and focus on my breathing as I continue. 'The next 72 hours passed, and Daniel had his beautiful hair gone, all shaved off. A massive bandage around his head with a drain cord to drain the fluid and to monitor the pressure in his skull.

It was just so sad, looking at Daniel he was just a shell. There was no response, no life in him. It felt like his soul had already left him. For three days following, we took turns to sit with him, talk to him. I got Jared home twice in those three days to shower and get rest. I'd cook something when I was home, even if it was just a pasta or some soup and take it in to the hospital so we could eat something warm and homemade.'

'Jared had about four hours sleep one time when we came home. It was going into the fourth day since the accident. He showered and had a renewed purpose. I didn't know what was going on he just seemed different. He came out of the spare bedroom and came downstairs, asked me if I was ready to go back to the hospital with him. I said of course I was. I put my arm on his shoulder and asked if everything was alright. "Yes. I've decided on something and would like you there please." That was all he said. We made small talk on the way to the hospital, but I never asked what the decision was. I knew he wanted to tell or say it to everyone involved at the same time.'

'We parked the car and started the walk into the hospital. He stopped and took my hand, "thank you for everything Annie, thank you for being here. Thank you. I have to do this, and I need to be strong, I know it's the right thing to do." He spoke with apprehension undercoated with knowing. He turned and walked towards the hospital doors. Stopping again and taking a breath and reaching out to grab my hand; we walked into the hospital.'

CHAPTER TWENTY-EIGHT

Annie

'We got up to intensive care where Bob and Lorraine were with Daniel. Both holding Daniel's hands, reciting stories about what he was like as a child. They looked exhausted. The ventilator beeping in the background; the nurse sitting near the doorway. We got to know all the nurses, and they were all so very nice with us. We sat with Bob and Lorraine for a little while, respectful of the policy of only two visitors at a time. After about ten minutes, Jared asked us if we minded giving him time with Daniel on his own and asked me to call his parents for them to come to the hospital. Of course, we were going to give him time and I kissed Jared on the top of his head, told him we would be in the waiting room when he wanted us.'

'Jared came out about an hour later, eyes red and swollen from crying. The nurse looking after Daniel had red eyes from crying also and she rushed past into what I assume was a staff room. Then a charge nurse came and said to Jared that the room was ready. We had no idea what was going on; we followed Jared into another room where the intensive care specialist, the surgeon and another woman I recognised seeing the day before all were waiting. The specialist explained they had performed tests on Daniel and done another CT scan and Daniel had no brain function; he was brain dead. The ventilator was keeping him alive. Jared looked at everyone with his eyes resigned to the fact he would never have his Daniel back. He had made a decision, after talking to Bob and Lorraine, to take Daniel off life support system but not before donating his organs to people who needed them. That was when this other woman spoke up; she was the coordinator for transplant retrievals. Jared and Daniel's parents decided to allow all but his corneas to be allocated to donors in need. Jared said there was always something about Daniel's eyes and knew it was irrational, but he couldn't do it. The coordinator was very reassuring, saying they don't push people into donating anything they didn't feel comfortable with. They just offered them information and left it with the families to decide.'

'So, that night we said our goodbyes to Daniel. People from Daniels office came to say goodbye, his friends and even some of the kids from the drop-in centre. A group of about fifteen of them. They had each other for support. Jared wanted them to say their goodbyes if they felt up to it. They came in about four at a time and the nurses let the rules bend a bit and Jared gave everyone support. Even at this difficult time, he was consoling them, they tried to be strong, but they were kids. Such an impressive bunch of kids. Kids that Jared and Daniel helped through difficult time. After we said our goodbyes, Jared sat with Daniel. We gave them privacy, even the nurse left the room. Jared came out a while later and said the team were going to take him down to theatre. "Let's go home, there's nothing more we can do here." We all thanked everyone in the unit, leaving a stream of tears behind us as we walked out.'

'It was strange and surreal; I don't know how to describe it. Not emotionless, numb in a way. Everyone trying to come to terms with the enormity of what had just happened in their own way. I knew I had to be on my own for a while. The past days had been a roller coaster of emotions. I hugged Jared who had his parents and Daniel's parents there, and brothers and sisters from both sides of their families… and now we were all left to move on without Daniel… and that was just what it was.'

Tears stream down Sophie's face. I've never told anyone about Daniel's passing before, never felt close enough to anyone to tell them. Sophie wanted to know. Although, I don't think she could have expected the reason why Jared hadn't dated for five years to be so powerful.

CHAPTER TWENTY-NINE

Annie

'Honey, it's one in the morning! I'm so sorry I didn't realise the time. Hugo is going to worry that you're still out and you have a bit of a drive home.' Sophie looks at me and smiles, the smile where all I see are her eyes sparkling. 'What? What are you smiling at?'

'Do you realise what you just called me?' Sophie says with a tinge of excitement.

I pause; 'Honey?' I answer. 'You don't like it? Shit! Sorry. I won't call you that again.'

'No, I loved it. No one has called me that in a very long time, it's sweet.' Sophie looks at her phone and starts to send a text. 'Well, Hugo's not concerned, there's been no messages from him and besides, if you don't mind, I'd like to stay. It took a lot to tell me about Daniel and Jared. I just want to be with you tonight. Is that alright? I've texted Hugo to tell him I've had too much to drink so will be staying at a friend's and I'll see him in the morning.'

I make my way to her and wrap my arms around her waist. 'I'd love you to stay, nothing would make me happier.'

Although happy she is staying, I'm not comfortable with the lies she tells. Is he not suspicious? Has she often stayed out? It seems like it was nothing for her to text Hugo with such a blatant lie; no guilt even crossed her face. I push the thought away as we go upstairs to my bedroom, holding hands, not saying anything. I love our physical contact; the soft touching and caressing we create by the purity of our instincts alone. It makes me feel close to her.

Lying on our backs, still holding hands, Sophie turns to look at me. 'That was hard for you to share, wasn't it?'

'Yes and no. No, because it was good to tell someone Daniel's story, and yes, because it felt like I was reliving it all over again. It's been five years but feels like it was yesterday. Thank you for listening to me and for not stopping me, even when I was crying. I think you knew I needed to get it out, I needed to say it.' I kiss her, whispering, 'Thank you again.'

Sophie entwines her tongue around mine in a soft, loving kiss. Sophie deepens the kiss. I want her so much. I want her to feel me. Sophie senses what I want, as she always does. 'I want to make love to you. I know I can't take away your pain, but tonight, I want you.' Her hand glides under my vest, where she finds my nipple and rolls it between her fingers, pulling on it. She has the softest fingers, the gentlest touch. She leans up to kiss me and I kiss her back, moaning.

'This little vest needs to come off I think,' she says as she tugs and pulls it up over my head, 'and these boy boxers will need to come off too. Mind you, I do admire your butt. I wanted to spank your arse as you walked by earlier,' Sophie says in a quiet, deep husky voice. Sophie kisses the corner of my mouth and skims her tongue over my cheek to my ear where she nibbles on my earlobe with playful joy; all the time her finger still plays with my nipple. She peppers kisses down my neck, down my chest, and comes to rest on my other nipple. Sophie tugs on one with her fingers while her wet tongue is working its magic on my other. I writhe in absolute bliss. I could explode right now.

Her hand snakes its way down to my centre, the moisture pooling between my legs as they open to allow her access. I want her fingers inside me and she glides two into me with methodical precision and enough force to push them deeper. Taking her time to part my tightness, she starts a rhythm inside me and I thrust forward to meet her in sync, grinding into her hand. I feel my walls tighten. Sophie stops, a cheeky grin on her face.

'Please, jeez, not a… whoa!' She starts making small circular motions on a spot I didn't know existed. 'Oh… God… What are…' are all the words I can muster as I feel a sensation I have never felt before. I feel my entire body about to explode. This one is different, an orgasm that my complete body will experience. 'Don't stop. Whatever it is don't… Ohhhhh fuck!' My body starts to tingle from the toes, upwards, pulsating and shattering around Sophie's fingers. Sophie sucks on my nipple with tenderness, bringing another shockwave pulsating through my body. Without hurry, she removes her fingers. I grab her hand as she brings her fingers to my mouth where I taste myself. 'Mmmmm, you have the best fingers. Magic fingers, in fact. I love these fingers.'

Sophie stops and looks deep into my eyes, puts her finger under my chin and turns my head towards hers, 'I love you, Annie. I am so in love with you. I haven't been in love before now. I love you so much.'

I stop, not believing what I heard.

'Don't just stare at me, say something. Anything?'

I smile at Sophie, 'I've been in love with you since the moment I saw you at the gallery. Sophie, I love you too, with all my heart.' I kiss her sweet lips and my eyes are heavy. 'I love you, Sophie Williams,' I whisper as I feel the warm embrace of Sophie's arms around me like a blanket.

'And I love you, Annie Mitchell,' Sophie says as she kisses the top of my forehead and sleep falls over us both.

Sophie

I was trembling with nervous excitement when I said those three little words. What if Annie didn't feel the same way? But before I had a chance to overthink it, I said it. There was no taking it back, it was out there. Annie's smile was genuine and her words heartfelt when she said it back.

Will this change things? It doesn't mean Annie expects me to move in, does it? I don't know anything about lesbians. Maybe it is too soon for me to say it. Maybe I shouldn't have said it. Did I push Annie into saying it? I'm not a lesbian though. I'm a woman who is in love with another woman. Society always puts people in boxes, or has to label everything. There are no boxes or labels here. I'm in love with Annie, the person, not the sex of the person, nothing more nothing less.

'What are you thinking Sophie? You're frowning. What's wrong, baby? You regret what you said?' Annie says, concern etched in her voice, bringing me back down to earth. How does she do that? Pick up when I'm worried or concerned about something.

'No. Yes. No!' I stumble over my words. 'No. I don't regret anything,' I defend. 'I don't know how this works. I told you I loved you, but now I don't know what you expect from me. I can't move in with you straight away. I'm just not sure how this works in your world.'

Annie kisses the tip of my nose. 'How it works is we keep doing what we're doing. There will come a time when we have to choose and we'll choose together. You're not on your own here. Tonight, let's enjoy us. You love me, I love you, but that doesn't mean we have to move in. There's no secret handshake, there's no rules because I love you and nothing needs to change. I often wonder, what does the rest of society thinks lesbians do when they love each other?' Annie reassures me, knowing my life is a little complicated at the moment. Am I making it complicated? Do I overthink it to complicate my life? I'm unsure. Changes? One thing I'm sure of is my love for Annie. That much I know is true.

CHAPTER THIRTY

Annie

I wake up dazed, disorientated, and horny. It takes me a few minutes to realise what's happening. Lying with my eyes closed, I feel Sophie sucking on my nipple. For a while I pretend to still be asleep, enjoying the sensation, feeling the pleasure of her, as she bites and pulls on my nipple. I hear Sophie moan, and it makes me smile and gets me that little bit more amorous. I give the game away as she bites a little bit harder making me moan. Sophie has my undivided attention and I'm awake, wide awake. I have missed waking up to some morning loving.

I lift Sophie's chin towards me and kiss her. Sophie is one superb kisser; from the first time I kissed her she has never held back, never hesitated. She snakes her way down my abdomen with kisses along the way, sliding up to play with my nipples again, she then slides into my crotch, her breath hot against my sensitive skin as she begins nuzzling into my pubic hair. Sophie glides a little further and inhales.

'Lift your bottom a bit please.' Sophie looks up at and into my hooded eyes. 'Put the pillow under your bottom? I may need a little help here,' Sophie says with a slight blush as I comply.

Once comfortable, she resumes her amazing caressing of my warm, moist vagina. Her tongue feels amazing as it finds my engorged pleasure point; her tongue makes circular motions with just the perfect pressure. I thrust my hips into Sophie's lavishing tongue, a natural instinct as we move and grind together. Sophie slows as she flicks my clit with abrupt bursts of delectable pleasures. It surprises me as I am hit with shockwave after shockwave of pleasure from her small flicking tongue.

I cannot control the full body sensations and let out a long loud moan. I feel Sophie smiling as she continues to pleasure me with an unrelenting enjoyment. I feel my orgasm building at a rapid pace as her tongue works her magic. One hand moves to play with my own nipple as my other hand goes to the top of Sophie's head and applies pressure downward. She complies with harder teasing of my clit. I can feel myself tingling as a huge build explodes over Sophie and my juices flow, saturating her chin.

I pull Sophie up on top of me. Skin to skin, as I shiver at her touch, I grab onto Sophie's arse. 'Now, that's what I think is a unique way of saying good morning darling, and what a splendid way to wake up.' I kiss Sophie hard and use my tongue to clean my juice from her chin. 'You can wake me up like that anytime you want.'

'I've never wanted anyone as much as I want you. I've never woken up so amorous before. I was so wet. I just wanted you. I knew you were sleeping, I'm sorry,' Sophie says with a rather cheeky grin on her face.

I roll Sophie over so I am straddling her thighs and hold her hands above her head. 'You're not sorry at all.'

'No, I'm not. I wanted to wake you and make love to you.

So, no, I'm not sorry,' Sophie says pleased with herself and her choice to pleasure me this morning.

'Well, I guess I'll have to punish you for waking me up. You know I love my sleep and you woke me,' I say, tickling her side.

'No, no, no! Please don't. Noooo! I'm sorry!'

Sophie and I wrestle on the bed, tickling, laughing. We stop, our eyes close, her breathe on mine, she moves her mouth closer to me ear, 'I do love you. I've never—' Sophie's phone ringing breaks the proclamation. 'Sorry,' Sophie says with sadness etched on her face.

'Hello, Sophie speaking.' Sophie listens to the voice on the other end of the phone. 'Of course, I'll be there, Em. I'll be home soon. Of course, I didn't forget. I'll leave here in fifteen minutes.' Another pause in the conversation, 'Where was I last night? Ahhh, I had drinks after work at Annabelle's and I didn't feel comfortable driving. I did text your father last night. He and Adrian went out? Okay darling, I should be there in forty five minutes at the latest. No later, I promise. Of course, we'll go to the shop where you saw the dress. I know I said it was expensive, but I know how much you love it. See you soon. Love you too darling.'

Sophie hangs up the phone. I get in first before she can say anything, I can see guilt written all over her face. 'Sounds like you're going dress shopping with a teenager. You *are* a brave woman,' I joke, trying to keep the atmosphere light, but I am failing.

'My niece is getting married and Emily saw this dress. At the time, I said it was too expensive for what it was, but the more I thought about it the more I knew it was perfect for Emily. To be fair she has done her homework and searched the internet looking for a cheaper version. I think guilt will get the better of me today and I'll get her what she likes,' Sophie rambles. Guilt for her daughter being neglected and for her own selfish desires to be happy with me. I find myself in love with her even more.

'I never want you to feel guilty, I'm so sorry, Sophie,' I assure her.

'No, it's not you. Hugo knew I wasn't coming home last night but didn't say anything to Emily this morning. Just said he didn't know where I was. He and Adrian have gone shopping for their suits and left Pebbles on her own.'

'Pebbles? Is that her nickname?'

'Yeah, she got that a lot as a kid. When we used to go to the seaside Emily would always come back with as many pebbles as she could carry. Adrian was about four and one day he said, "You love pebbles, I'm going to call you Pebbles", so she was Pebbles from that day, till she hit senior school then she claimed she was far too mature to have such a juvenile nickname. Although, I'm sure she secretly still likes it. She knows when I call her Pebbles, she's on a winner with whatever she wants. I think that will be today.'

'Do I make you feel guilty about us, together like this?' Sophie stops me.

'No. You make me feel alive. You make me feel desired and loved, so very loved. Guilty no. I should have the guts to walk away from my loveless marriage. Hugo and I are just two people living together in a house and are both as miserable as each other but cannot admit it. I don't think the kids see it as we try put on a brave face. In the bedroom, we sleep with our backs to one another and as far away from each other as possible. I'd move into the spare room but the kids would start to question everything, and I'm not quite ready for that conversation just yet. Sorry, I should go…'

'Have a shower first and freshen up. Grab a pair of knickers out of my drawer and put yours in the washing basket. Can't carry dirty knickers in your handbag,' I wink at Sophie, 'and you can't pull them out to pay for Pebbles' dress.'

'You're incorrigible you know that. Thank you for everything. I'll just have a quick shower.' Sophie turns to go then turns back, 'I love you.'

'I love you too. Now shower.'

A few minutes later Sophie comes downstairs. 'I wish I had time for…' she starts as I hand her a travel mug of fresh coffee. 'You are amazing. Thank you, I have to go. I'm sorry, Annie.'

'It's fine and thank you for staying last night. It was nice to wake up knowing you were there, especially *there!*' I say with a smirk remembering the morning's awesome event. 'Oh, and here's some breakfast to go. Ham and cheese toastie, it should stay warm enough.'

'You think of everything. Thank you again. I'll have to dash, talk to you tonight?'

'Of course. I'll walk you to your car.'

One last kiss at the door then she drives away.

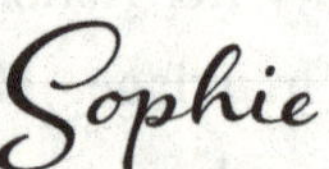

I can't keep my hands off Annie; even asleep I wanted her. I love how we fell asleep holding each other. When I'm with her, I sleep so sound. I crave her, though it took me an hour to work up enough courage to do what I dreamed of doing, I managed to leave it until a reasonable hour before I couldn't hold out any longer. To make a woman orgasm is the ultimate aphrodisiac. I made myself wet waking Annie up. I could wake up every morning like that with her.

I push those thoughts out of my head as I drive home to pick up Emily. *Where is my life heading?* My mind is working overtime. I'm nervous as I imagine a future that may be possible yet the beat of my heart fastens and my breath tightens in my chest as I think of what can happen. I don't want to hurt my family, but more importantly, the dryness in my throat and ache in my heart is caused by the idea of not fully being with Annie sooner. What if she gets sick of waiting for me to leave Hugo? She knows I can't leave just yet, not with the children. She will wait. Or will she? I can't help but to smile when I finish the last of the toastie Annie made me. She's so thoughtful, and sweet. I have to find my courage and be the person I want her to be proud of, and soon.

CHAPTER THIRTY-ONE

Annie

When Sophie drives off, I wander back into the house. It feels empty. I've always loved this house, when Sophie is here it feels like a home. She has a beautiful energy that emits from within and surrounds her, and that emanates through my house. I love it when she's here, but she has a husband and children. Children who need parents, however unhappy they are. How can I break that up? I can't. It's not fair to any children.

What does Sophie want? She says she loves me, but is what we have enough to prepare her to leave her husband or children? Can she make a life with a woman? Could I share my life with her children? What if the children take sides and refuse to have anything to do with their mother because of me? Will Sophie stay in the marriage to protect her children from being bullied because of the scandal that might arise?

I'm ahead of myself here, it's only been about six months. If she leaves him, Sophie will need time on her own and in her own her space. I'm not being a part of that old lesbian joke, *"what does a lesbian bring on a second date? A suitcase."*

In the short time I've known her, she occupies my thoughts

for what feels like, twenty-four hours a day. I go to sleep thinking about her, I wake up and my first thought is her. I never tire of talking with her, we share the same views on most things and we don't always agree but we have lively discussions. How would I feel if I didn't have Sophie in my life? Even after this brief time, it would be cold and I would be in a place of unbearable loneliness. I have flourished in the last few years on my own, so it wouldn't be the end of the world, but I want Sophie to be in that world. Can I share her with her husband and children for the next few years? That is something I need to think long and hard about. But first, I need to change those bedsheets.

CHAPTER THIRTY-TWO

Annie

Sophie texts me later in the evening, asking if I have time to talk; I always have time for her. I would drop everything for this woman who has captured my heart. Sophie picks up on the second ring. 'Hello Annie. How was the rest of your day?'

'Well after I changed the sheets and put on fresh ones.'

'Oh dear. I'm sorry. I… I… gosh I am a bit embarrassed.'

I laugh as a woman of forty-four has such an adorable innocence and I can picture her blushing on the other end of the phone. 'Come on, don't get all bashful now. It's okay. Next time you can wash the sheets before you leave.' We both laugh and it feels right. 'Where in the house are you?'

'In the office. Why?' Sophie asks with trepidation.

'Are the kids busy? Is Hugo occupied?"

'Yes. And yes.' She answers with further suspicion.

'Well, I want you to lock the door. I don't want us to be interrupted.'

'What are you up to?' On her end, I hear the sound of a door closing and lock snibbing. 'I'm feeling a bit nervous…'

'Stop with these questions, you'll find out.' I bite my lip with my own anticipation and hopefulness that she will play along with me. 'Now, make yourself comfortable.'

'I'm in my chair, I'm comfortable. What are you up to, Miss?'

'I don't think I had the pleasure of reciprocating the favour from this morning and I'd like to rectify that. I want to make you feel as good as I felt this morning,' I say in a hushed tone. I hear the change in Sophie's breathing and her voice drops slightly deeper. 'Can you undo your bra for me? Now I know you've got one on because you've just come in, it will make what we're about to do easier.'

'It's undone,' Sophie says breathless with excitement.

'Now, with your right hand, move it under your shirt and play with your nipple,' I whisper. 'Scrape your fingertips over and back again. Feel your nipple growing under your fingertips. Just keep doing that… back and forth. Now imagine me biting your other nipple, my tongue teasing your areola. I'm working my way from the outside in. My breath hot on your flesh. My wet tongue flicking and licking your hard nipple. Can you feel it?' I ask.

'Yes. Yes, I can feel you,' Sophie purrs and I hear her groan into the mouthpiece of the phone, a long-drawn-out moan

'Shhh, you have to be quiet. I haven't finished with you yet. Now, find the button on your jeans. Undo your button, pull your zipper down…' I listen to her zipper being lowered and let my imagination paint the beautiful picture of Sophie spread in her chair and jeans lowered. 'Slide your hand down into your underwear. Are you wet? I think you are. I hear your breathing. It's fast and shallow. I can almost hear your heart beating. Tell me how wet you are.'

'Very. I'm so wet…' Sophie purrs in delight.

'How many fingers are you using? You like two fingers. You like it when I pump two fingers into your wet pussy. Slide your own fingers in and taste yourself… Sweet, aren't you?'

'Mmmmm.' It's the only noise Sophie can muster.

'Now find your beautiful clit. I want slow circular movements; delicate as though caressing a flower… Not too hard… don't come too quick, enjoy it. I'm enjoying it, making love to you this way. I want to make love to you every way I can. My fingers are playing with your nipple. I'm playing with your left nipple. Now… apply a little more pressure. A little faster. You want to come, don't you? You're close… How close are you?'

'Very… Very… close.'

'Now I'm biting your nipple. You love it when I bite your nipple. You're close to that orgasm and when I bite your nipple it sends you over the edge. Come for me.' I pause. 'I want to hear you come.'

Sophie moans into the phone, exploding with a loud blended moan and groan at once. Hearing Sophie orgasm sends me into orbit as I explode seconds after her. I almost dropped the phone as my body trembles with pleasure fuelled spasms.

Sophie and I listen to each other breathing for long moments after; both of us returning to reality in our own time.

'That was unexpected. And what a way to finish a day. You never cease to amaze me. Expect the unexpected right?' Sophie purrs like a well-fed cat on a comfy pillow.

'Absolutely,' I say smiling and enjoying the lingering of bliss between us.

'Mmmmm. Thank you.'

'My pleasure. Literally, my pleasure.'

'I can't remember what I was ringing you for.' We laugh as I hear a voice in the background calling out.

'Mum, where are you? I need my shirt for tomorrow and I can't find it.'

'I think that's my time up,' Sophie says with dutiful closure. 'Thank you, I can face anything now, even those dreaded school lunches.'

'Bye Sophie.'

'Bye Annie.'

'I love you,' we say in unison as we hang up.

Sophie

It takes me a minute to compose myself and readjust my clothing, smiling the entire time. I hear the office door rattle as someone tries to open it.

'Sophie why is the door locked?' I hear Hugo's voice as I open the door.

'I was searching for birthday presents and I didn't want the kids to barge in,' I whisper to Hugo as I let him in. *Another lie. Will it ever stop?*

'Em did you find the shirt?' I ask.

'Yeah, I've ironed it thanks. Adrian's shirt and school pants are also. All done Mum, why don't you sit and relax.'

This night gets better, although nothing beats what happened earlier.

'You okay Mum?'

'Yes, darling why?'

'I don't know, you look…' Emily pauses, trying to find words, 'you look relaxed, happy I guess…'

'It was a lovely surprise, ironing the uniforms like that,' I answer with pride and she stands a bit taller in front of me.

'Must do it more often.' She laughs and kisses me and Hugo and then moves away.

'I'm off to bed. Love you, Mum. Night, Dad.'

'Love you darling. Sleep well.'

CHAPTER THIRTY-THREE

Annie

I lie awake through the night my mind flipping in thoughts of Sophie and me. Will we ever have a future together? Perhaps she is comfortable in the heterosexual realm. After all, she says she has often been attracted to women in her life but never acted on anything. Really, we know little of each other's world's. I was born gay and it's all I have ever known and even though I have slept with men, there was no emotion. I was trying to fit in. Thank goodness I came to my senses, became strong enough to stand up and say, *"this is how I will live my life, true to myself."* This is my normal, nothing queer about it. People say I had a choice and if I had chosen to be a heterosexual maybe my life could have been easier for my family to accept, instead of struggling with the concept. Maybe it would be easier without all the questions when men find out I am a lesbian. Maybe easier without the sexual innuendos and fighting the causes for our equal rights, back when they entitled us to equal rights and refused to grant them to us. Years ago, Jenny would've had no say in my medical treatment or wishes had I become ill and she was my partner. They would have gone to a blood relative, even if that relative knew nothing of my wishes. Because Jenny was not related, she had no say in my care. The fight was worth it, we got our rights, or at least some of them.

But it's not always about choosing the easier path, it's about being true to who you are and not being swayed. My parents' words ring in my head, *"go straight or move out..."* I knew I could never turn back, even if it meant losing my parents support and love. Can Sophie choose her path as I chose mine? Maybe it is harder to change as you become older? Will it be right for Sophie to choose this lifestyle with me? She says her marriage with Hugo is loveless, but does she want to leave the security behind? Sophie said she loved me. I am an everyday, ordinary person who goes about with modest goals and lives with simple hopes and dreams. Will I be able to share my world with her?

Annie

I'm back to work on Monday when Jared phones. 'Got time for a quick catch up today. I'm so sorry. I feel I have neglected you. So, lunch today?'

'I'd love to, but I may not be able to get away till two,' I say. 'Does that fit your work schedule?'

'Perfect. See you at two,' he affirms and we both hang up.

*

Lunch rolls around and we meet at our usual place.

'Tell me, how are things with you and Marcus?' I ask, hoping it's going well.

'Annie, I can't believe I've found someone after all this time. He's everything I thought I'd never have again. I feel like pinching myself. It's been so long since… Daniel but… I don't compare Marcus to Daniel. I'll always love Daniel, but I know I've found someone who shares my passion and has a lovely family, not to mention who are so proud of him and his art.'

'You've met the family? Not all at once I hope!?'

'Yes! It was a nephew's birthday and there was an enormous family gathering. All the family were there. His parents, brother, sisters, cousins, everyone! And they made me feel very welcome. I felt I was intruding on the party, but they are so gracious, and they said Marcus hasn't stopped smiling since we'd met. His father took me aside, and I thought here it comes with the *"I'm not happy about my son being gay scenario"* but I had it all wrong. He told me he saw a gentleman and that he liked me and that was enough for him. Shook my hand and welcomed me to his family.'

'Oh, Jared that is so sweet,' I say as tears welled in my eyes. 'Can I ask something?'

'I'm never sure what you are going to ask, but it never stops you. Go right ahead.' Jared laughs and tilts his head. I smile at his relaxed candour; it has been a while since he has been like this and I bask in his presence.

'It's been a few months,' I say with a tentative voice.

'Yesss,' Jared responds, drawing out the word.

'Do you think you could fall in love?'

'Do I think I could fall in love with him? Are you serious?'

I nod in reflex to his questions. He laughs and slaps his hand on the table, hard enough to bounce the cutlery. 'I already have,' Jared answers with a broad grin, 'And I've told him so; I said the L word one night. Let me think back…' Jared pauses, his smile beaming with a contagion that it seems to have spread throughout the entire cafe. 'It was about three weeks ago. Three weeks tomorrow, if we're keeping track. I told him first.'

'Really? Gigantic step for you J.'

'I know, but it felt right, you know. Having Marcus in my life is just so awesome and I thought it might scare him away for saying it, but it was a perfect. Whenever something feels right, you have to tell them you love them.'

'And Marcus's response?' I say. The smile on Jared's face expands further and his eyes light up like they're electrified.

He says, 'He told me he'd fallen in love with me long before I even admitted it. He was scared, also, can you believe that? I mean, he knew my history with Daniel and the horrible past few years I have had to survive, and I've been very honest with him about my past. About everything…'

'Are we having a housewarming party anytime soon?' I prompt in excitement.

'No.'

'No?!' I exclaim with false hurt. He leans over the table and kisses my cheek. He just will not stop smiling. I feel so elated for his happiness and in my mind say a prayer for blessing of his beautiful soul to stay so alive and bask in this new love for a long time.

'Well not yet, but I did ask him to move in,' Jared says and emphasises a huge gulp and rolls his eyes like a madman. I laugh at his delightful animations. 'He stays over some weekends and then a couple of days during the week. He doesn't want to spoil things either by moving too quick; he's scared the bubble will burst. Plus, he doesn't want to live in the house without contributing. He knows I own it but he would like to contribute, I respect that. Maybe down the track when he's a better-established artist around the world or even the universe, I mean he is so talented… and he will sell painting after painting but he feels now he is a mere struggling painter, his words not mine. He will in time feel comfortable with living together, and perhaps buying something bigger where he could have an awesome studio.' Jared speaks in colours and lights, as though he is painting a picture of himself in a life he has been dreaming of for so long.

'I went over to the studio he rents now. He gets so absorbed and in the zone when he paints, music blaring the same song over and over. I just sat on a stool in the corner watching him immersed in it all that he didn't even notice me for about twenty minutes. I moved, and he saw that out of the corner of his eye. Scared the life out of him, and me!' He chuckled in memory and I could see it rerunning through his eyes.

I smiled and asked. 'How's the painting going? Any more work come through?'

'He sold everything from the show and got some commissions to do others. There is some talk of a couple of big corporations doing refurb's and they want him and Ben, another artist, to do some work for them. Nikki, the curator, put him in touch with people, plus the journalists who covered the opening wrote up his work. In short, it's all going freaking awesome. But?' Jared pauses and his big eyes drop with an obvious ongoing hesitation.

'It's going to be fine, Jared. Don't worry, you deserve this and nothing bad will happen. Please, relax,' I assure with a big-sisterly smile and nod of confidence.

'I hope so,' he sighs. 'I've been scared to be happy with someone else. I think that's why I have avoided a relationship. I couldn't deal with losing someone I love again, and I haven't been ready to move on. I can't lose Marcus; he's too important to me. I love him and I want to make a life with him; so yes, we're going to make a life together I declare it now!' Jared exhales as if all the fear he's been holding in for five long years has been released into the air about him and no longer hinders his soul.

'Should I keep my eye out for the perfect house for you both? Something with a yard and a shed out the back for the studio.' I make light of the moment and Jared relaxes into it with me. 'I know you will want the conservatory,' I say meaning every word hidden under my mockery to give him the push he needs.

Jared laughs. 'You just want a sale. Always working, you are. Seriously though, if you see something let me know. If it's meant to be it will pop up at the right moment,' he says and I couldn't be happier for him.

'So, your turn…' he says as he leans across the table onto his forearms. 'Tell me about your lady love, how's it going? Any sign of her leaving her marriage and venturing over to the rainbow side?' Jared says with a wink.

'Ahh yes, the marital home with the obnoxious husband and two children. The husband being the obnoxious one, not the teenage children although I'm sure teenagers can be obnoxious at times. Two teenage children who may not like to see their mother with another woman instead of their father. The mother that seems afraid of being seen out with me, or telling friends she's attracted to a woman in case she loses them? That one?'

'She's said all that?' Jared exclaims, almost shouting it out.

'No, that is all of my own anxiety rearing its ugly head. I'm just worried it's going to backfire. Maybe I'm just a game.'

'Do you really want to think that?'

My phone beeps and I read it, 'No. Yes. I don't know. Sorry, J, got to dash my three thirty appointment's waiting. I didn't realise the time.' I get up from the table and kiss Jared on the top of his head.

'You go, I've got this, and don't think this conversation is over.'

'Thank you, and I know you won't let it.' I race out of the cafe, trying to clear my head to focus on what is important to my survival: my job. I'm relieved to be called away from Jared as I am not ready to talk about the real source of my fear in relation to Sophie's non-commitment: I'm in love with her like no one I have known before and I might lose her anyway.

CHAPTER THIRTY-FOUR

Annie

Home at last. My last appointment went longer than expected and the clients were demanding about their apartment details and being obtuse to the market-values, not to mention they kept trying to hammer my commission down. I open the fridge and seek the chilled bottle of wine; I snatch a glass from the sink rack and move to the lounge. My mobile rings because the office phone is still diverted; I answer it without looking at the screen, my mind scattered. *Please don't let it be the home owners again, I can't deal with it now,* I think.

'Good evening, Annette Mitchell speaking.'

I hear Sophie laughing on the other end of the phone and a relaxed wave of joy falls over me. 'You've had an awful day, haven't you?'

'Not so much day, just afternoon. Frustrating as hell,' I say, pouring myself a glass of wine and slipping off my shoes; another wave of relief flows over me and I sigh. 'And how can you tell I've had a terrible day?'

'Your tone is more businesslike and I know you're frowning when you speak.' I scoff at this, both surprised and flattered by the fact she has picked up on my subtleties. 'I seem to be able to pick up on these little idiosyncrasies now and I don't even think you know you're doing it half the time.'

'Anyway, enough about me,' I snap. 'How was your day? The professor still away?'

'Yes, in Italy presenting papers. He'll be there for another few weeks. It's been good with him away. It's allowed me to catch up on work. Although he emails me when wanting certain papers emailed. He never stops, that man. He sent me red wine from a boutique winery he passed and said it will never be available for sale in retail shops. Brewed for some Prince in some far Eastern European country. It will be perfect in twelve months… blah, blah, anyway, what I'm ringing for is to see if you're free tomorrow afternoon?' she asked direct and sure. I gave a shake of my head in surprise. 'I'm taking the afternoon off and I want to see if I can find a dress for this wedding. It's formal and I haven't got anything suitable. I'd like to find something I can feel comfortable in while still exuding glamour and class, you know…' and she laughed in such a way I would have kissed her mouth so hard if she was here with me.

'I think I can wing that seeing as I'm the boss,' I answer. 'I'm in trouble if I can't. Hang on, let me just check my appointments.' I flip pages in my organiser to check for any meetings. 'Nothing, that's perfect, have you got anywhere to start in mind?'

'I've got a few places. They're not far from your office. How about I swing by and pick you up?'

'Sounds good. I'll be free from about twelve thirty.'

'I should be there by one, but if I'm going to be late, I'll call you.' She seems to be hurried. 'Sorry, I have to go. Hugo and the kids went out and bought dinner and I've just heard the car pull up. I'll see you tomorrow. Bye,' Sophie says and hangs up the phone, not even giving me a chance to say goodbye. I hold the phone to my ear for a moment, just listening to the silence, wondering if we'll ever have the life I crave. A life with Sophie, and even if teenage children are included, that's still what I want most.

CHAPTER THIRTY-FIVE

Annie

Sophie texts me at about ten minutes to from down the road. I give her directions to my office car park and suggest we use a cab to get about so we don't have to fuss over parking. She agrees and I call one to meet up with us at the car park. I greet her with a warm embrace and stand holding her for a few seconds, with the warmth of the sun on my back and the heat radiating from Sophie is wonderful, like I'm wrapped in a warm cocoon. The cab arrives. I open the door for Sophie, and she slides across the opposite side of the cab allowing me to jump in. The ride is brief, and we hold hands and smile as we make small talk. We hop out of the cab in the main street where the best retail shops are found and wander in and out of a few dress shops until we stumble across one where we like several of the dresses in the window. 'This could be fruitful,' I say and we enter. 'I like the look of these.'

Sophie and I pick out half-a-dozen or so dresses. 'You always seem to pick out the dark colours. I love the bold and brighter colours on you,' I say, flicking through her pile of dresses. She glances at me and raises an eyebrow. 'Humour me by trying on these. Please?'

'Of course, I'll try them on but remember it's a wedding, not Mardi Gras,' Sophie says with a wry smile on her face. I usher us into the change room which is just smaller than my office.

'They haven't skimped on the space in these fitting room,' I say. 'I'll wait outside, I want to see them on, even if you may not like them. Of course, I'm talking about the one's I picked. Leave the ones you picked aside, okay?'

Sophie tries on a couple, and they look amazing in my eyes. But she is particular and doesn't like the bright colours. It's as if she doesn't want to stand out or have attention directed at her.

'What do you think of this one?' Sophie asks stepping out of the dressing room and looking in the mirror. She turns and faces me. 'Well, what do you think?'

'Nice, very nice,' I say as I look over her figure, curved and voluptuous for a woman her age. Her body is full and firm and she holds her muscle tone well. Her eyes wear her intelligence as much as her shoulders carry her postured beauty. I love her, it is again confirmed.

'The dress! Not my boobs!' she exclaims noticing my gaze.

'The dress is sexy too, but the cleavage is, wow!' Sophie's whole face light up as she smiles.

'Okay, enough… I'll try the next one on.' Sophie comes out of the change room after a few more minutes and she spins on the spot in a beautiful dress of red and lilac.

'It's nice but I liked the other one more, it showed off your curves.' I say, 'Reminded me of the dress you wore to the opening, but this one is more formal which is what you want I suppose…'

'You only liked it because it showed off my boobs.'

'What can I say? I'm a boob girl.' I wink at Sophie.

'You are incorrigible. Can you unzip me please, I don't want to damage it.'

'With pleasure,' I say, entering the change room behind her, we are facing the mirror. I start to unzip the dress, deliberately slow and teasing. Our lock eyes in the mirror and her blue eyes flicker with a sparkle of knowing.

'Don't even think about it,' Sophie says in a whisper of desire.

'What?' I ask, an innocent coyness in my smile. 'You asked me to help you, that's what I'm doing.' I unzip her dress all the way and slide her arms out of the dress with a long caressing of my soft hands; her skin is smooth and warm to touch. The dress slides to the floor.

'Oh my God, I love you in this colour, I say as I look down her body to see her in her underwear. 'You wore this for me, didn't you? This was deliberate, you want to drive me crazy. I love these French knickers.' I rub my finger along the inside of the waistband.

'Don't,' Sophie says in a hushed tone. We don't break eye contact, both looking at each other in the mirror. My left-hand glides to Sophie's bra strap, pulling it down in one movement, exposing her perfect breast. My fingers manoeuvre to find her nipple which I tease with great response. Sophie watches me in the mirror, mesmerised as her breath quickens.

'We shouldn't,' she whispers, 'we may get caught.'

I move close to her ear, and say, 'There's a lock on the door and I'm sure the salesgirl isn't going to come charging in. They knock first.'

Sophie shivers and goosebumps ripple over her arms like tiny pinpricks. I rest my chin on her right shoulder, not pausing our eye contact. My hand still playing with her nipple as I slide my other hand into her French panties to feel what I'm looking for within her wetness and apply pressure with my small circular motion on her pulsating clit. Our eyes lock together until Sophie lowers her gaze to watch my hand in her panties moving slightly. I can feel her gentle spasms against me and feel her breath quickening. Her eyes are mesmerised as she watches my hand grind her clit with my firm fingers against her pelvis. Her eyes blink and expand with desires of lust, a deeper hunger appears in her face and her tongue licks at her lips with an obvious craving. She realises she is going to watch herself come. Her breath quickens, sweat beads on her brow, her nipples erect between my fingers.

'I'm so close,' she purrs.

'I know,' I say. The view of Sophie exploring her desires in the mirror before us making me hunger too.

I whisper in her ear, 'I love fucking you… I love making you come. Anywhere, everywhere.' Sophie's eyes narrow as she bends her knees into my hand while I push up and she moves her hips in rhythm with my hand's motion. Her breath is fast and shallow now.

'S–s–s–s–so close.' Sophie stutters as trembling of pleasures rattle her muscles. 'Oh god yes, Annie…'

'I know. Come for me,' I say pinching Sophie's nipple harder. Her knees buckle further as her orgasm engulfs her body with a crippling bolt of euphoria she did not expect.

'My God, that was… That was… Ohh fuck.' I feel Sophie's body begin to relax as her orgasm rides out its wave of ecstasy. I kiss her shoulder when there is a knock on the door.

'Can I help you with anything? How's the size?' the sales

assistant calls from the other side of the door.

'No, I've got everything in hand thanks. The size is perfect, it's a sublime fit,' I answer and smile. Sophie's eyes open and her mouth drops open.

'Give me a shout if you need a hand, or another size,' the girl yells and leaves.

'We will, thanks,' I respond.

'I can't believe you said that.' Sophie feigns shock.

'What? I just told her we didn't need a hand. I had it all under control.' I can't help but smirk. 'That's payback.'

'Payback? Payback for what?' Sophie frowns with no disappointment at all.

'Don't bite the hand that fucked you. Now, best you get dressed, otherwise the sales assistant will think we've been up to no good.'

'I hate you.' Sophie laughs.

'I know. I'll meet you outside.' I leave the change room laughing, when I'm met by the young sales assistant. 'You don't have a bathroom I could use, do you? I just need to wash my hands. My fingers are a bit sticky.' I hear Sophie choke on her breath and call back to her sweetly, 'Are you alright Sophie? Do you need another hand?'

'NO! I'm fine. I'll be out shortly.'

'Restroom is just through there madam,' says the sales assistant with coy innocence; I see a slight smile on her lips. We make our way out of the shop after purchasing Sophie's dress. 'You never once made eye contact with the sales assistant and you were blushing throughout the whole transaction. She gave you a discount too. I'm shocked Sophie, that is not like you,' I scold her while fighting a smile.

'The discount is because she must have heard everything we were doing! I'm so embarrassed,' Sophie exclaims with a fit of giggles.

'No, you're not, you loved it.'

'I did. I feel so alive. I never know what to expect next.'

'Will we have a coffee?' I ask.

'No. Wine and a cigarette are needed to help me regain my composure from this amazing shopping experience…' Sophie declares out loud and with her arms spread apart.

'But you don't smoke,' I say with jest.

'After that, I definitely need one.'

We both laugh and seek out the nearest bar.

CHAPTER THIRTY-SIX

Sophie

It's Friday and I'm home from work. Annie has a convention for work this afternoon and drinks in the evening, something to do with the real estate institute. It's strange to be home early. I walk in to find Emily with books sprawled across the kitchen table as she studies, and a furrowed forehead, always a sign of her concentration since she was young.

'Hey Mum, I didn't expect you home so soon,' she says without looking up from her pages of books in front of her.

'I was about to say the same thing. Why are you home? I'm not complaining, it's nice to see you without the men being rowdy.'

'We had the last two lessons free, Miss Myers was off sick,' she explained. 'They had no one to cover so instead of studying in the library, I opted to come home. I knew it would be quiet here. I've got exams coming up. Oh, school rang Dad to see if it was alright. I knew it would be easier to get him at work than you.'

'That makes sense,' I concur as I move around her. 'I'll head upstairs darling, so I don't disturb you,' I say, kissing Emily's head as I pass her.

'No, stay down here. I'm due for a break,' she says, standing and stretching. 'I'll make us a cup of tea.'

'I've bought some cakes for the boys, but I think we'll have them instead.' I wink at Em as she gets up to put the kettle on. Emily hasn't eaten sweet things after six at night since she was about eight years old. We had issues with her becoming hyperactive and not sleeping if she had sweets in the evening. She's into the habit now and it's her choice. I'm sure she has outgrown the hyper stage, but I'm pleased knowing it's not anything to do with an eating disorder. We sit at the kitchen table enjoying our tea and some quality time together. I cherish the rare times I get to sit with my little girl and have an adult conversation with her. She is growing into a beautiful woman. She has a lovely disposition and I am proud of her. It's not all rosy though and we do clash at times. She is headstrong and will fight to the end if she thinks she is right, or something isn't fair. I love that about her. I love everything about her. I can see her being the eminent lawyer she wants to be.

'You go out Friday nights. Are you going out later?' Emily asks before she takes a sip of her tea.

'I wouldn't say I go out every Friday. I catch up with friends maybe on the odd Friday. Does it bother you that I'm out? And to answer your question, no, I'm not going tonight,' I say noticing a twinge of guilt wash over me. *Am I neglecting my children for Annie?*

'No! Not at all. You've been out a few times with the girls from work on a Friday but,' Emily pauses as if she's thinking how to pose the next question, 'I don't know… but you come home happier. I know that sounds weird and you've just had a great night with the girls, but you smile more, you're happier, you're not as irritable. Don't worry, I see how Dad treats you and talks to you but the past few months you've changed. I'm not saying anything was wrong with you before, you are just happier. Dad is a dick.'

'EMILY!'

'Mum, admit it and I'm not a kid anymore,' she says with a scowl. 'I see how he treats you and how he talks to you. I live here for god's sake. He doesn't have any respect for you anymore, and you, any woman, deserve respect. He gets me so angry at stupid crap. I love him, but I am not going to marry a man like him,' Emily says as she looks out the window for a minute then returns to look me in the eye. 'Are you having an affair with another man? I wouldn't blame you if you were.'

What can I say? I can't answer her; my mind has ceased functioning and I am frozen to the spot. She smiles at me with a sudden knowing as I have no defence to her assumption. 'No. No, Em I'm not having an affair with another man,' I ramble. It is *technically* the truth; Annie isn't a man.

'Well keep going out with your Friday night girls then. I love seeing my old Mum happier.' She shrugs and takes a bite of a coffee scroll, licking her mouth of icing. For the slightest moment she looks five years old again and my heart misses a beat. She has grown so fast; blossomed into a real woman. I sigh with an immense pride. Regardless of the life I live with Hugo, we've created a wonderful daughter.

'Enough of the old!' I scold with a grin.

'Okay, old girl,' Em laughs, 'but these women seem to agree with you. How come you're not going out tonight?'

I never want to lie to Emily, or anyone of my family, but I have no choice at the moment. 'One had a work thing she had to go to and some were just tired; big week. We'll catch up next week. Have you got much more study to do?' I ask in attempt to direct the conversation back to her and away from me.

'I think I'll do another hour and that will be it; give myself the night off and start again in the morning. Although I don't know why, Dad and Adrian will just be sitting in front of the television. Maybe we should do something?'

'Maybe we should,' I consider. 'What would you like to do? Go somewhere for dinner? See a movie? Anything you want within reason for this "old girl".'

'You're not really old. Well not that old,' Emily says and we both laugh. 'This may sound lame but you know what I'd love to do?'

'No idea.' I shake my head. 'But I dread the thought. Go on.'

'Remember years ago, we'd all go bowling?'

'Ten pin bowling?'

'No Mum, lawn bowling. Of course, ten pin! Sheesh!'

'Yes. You want to go bowling?'

'Yeah, it was so much fun. One of the happiest times I remember as a family. Even if Dad drank while we were there, he was funny. Remember the time he ran down the lane to try and get a strike because he was losing? And the ball still went in the gutter. And the time you fell on your butt after you let go of the ball and you got a strike!' Emily is laughing, tears cascading down her cheeks, recalling these bowling nights.

'Sure. Let's go but I will not be reliving those memories for you.' I think on what best to wear as the shoes in the alley never go with my outfits. 'Hot dogs and fries at the alley then?'

'Of course. The night wouldn't be the same without that. I am so going to beat you,' Emily says with a joy in her voice I had forgotten the sound of. I've missed time with Emily. I have an overwhelming sense of guilt. *But I only go out one night a fortnight. It's not every Friday night. And I only call into Annie's on the weekend when the kids are out. I'm not neglecting them.* I scold myself and my foolish guilt. There is no need for these feelings or am I projecting what will come when all this is destroyed by my selfishness for loving Annie?

The front door slams and a school backpack is thrown to a corner of the lounge as Adrian comes bouncing into the kitchen, straight for the fridge and not noticing Emily and I sitting at the table. He turns and exclaims in shock, 'Fuck. Shit. Sorry. Why didn't you say something! You scared me. I could have had a heart attack! You're both trying to kill me.'

'Language young man,' I say to be stern with him but we all burst out laughing. 'Emily and I are going bowling tonight. Do you want to join us?'

'Bowling? Lame. No thanks. Dad and I are watching a game tonight. But can you take me to Liam's tomorrow? Dad always makes me walk. What's for dinner tonight? Can we have pizza?'

'Emily and I are having dinner out, but I'll order pizza for you and your father before we go.'

'Cool,' Adrian says and proceeds to the lounge where he parks himself before the television and commences to channel surf.

'I booked us a lane. I thought it would be better than waiting for one,' says Emily as she puts her phone down. I shake my head and contemplate just how old I may be getting when my kids use technology like it is second nature and I can't even change my ringtone.

'Good planning,' I say as Emily packs up her books and I order Pizzas for my boys. We change into our casual alley clothes and Emily is bouncing with excitement I have not seen in her for a long time. Once ready, we head off to the bowling alley. 'Come on Pebbles, there's life left in the old girl. Game on.'

Sophie

The lanes are thumping with music and people everywhere as we walk up to the counter where Emily exudes confidence and speaks to the stressed-out teenager behind the counter, who asks our sizes and then gets us the obligatory bowling shoes, which I dread thinking on how many people have worn before us.

'Three games? You want to play three games?' the boy yells over the music. Emily spins to me with an excited grin.

'Oh, come on Mum, best of three. But I'm winning anyway so the third will be to give you a chance,' she says with certainty. I shake my head, guessing she gets the nonchalance from me.

'Game on, girl. And there is no way you're winning the first two games. Dream on.'

It's like old times as we laugh and mock and stir each other up, only now she is grown up and our humour has a certain adult undertone we haven't shared before and find I like it. The games smash past as ball after ball and laugh after laugh, we blur into the crowded alley with a natural relaxed enjoyment I cannot recall having for a long time. Two games are done when it feels like we just started playing.

'I thought you said you would take the first two games?' I mock. 'Hmmm, doesn't look like that's panned out for you. Third and decider. Game on.'

We finish the third game, Emily beating me by two points, and she is on a high and giving me a ribbing.

'Why do these shoes always have to be so rank? I feel I need to soak my feet in anti-bacteria wash when I finish.' Emily cringes as she holds them out in front of her and drops them to the floor. 'Thanks Mum, this was great,' Emily says as she hugs me and there are tears in our eyes and we smile in a moment we have not shared before like this. I feel we are friends.

We take our shoes up to the counter where a few people wait for the same. Emily is still smiling and giggling. I am beaming with joy that we had this time together. I do not even notice the people about us, it is our world right now and nothing else can matter. Just then, the woman in front of us spins and runs straight into me. I half expected to be wearing a sudden cold cup of coke over my front. But instead, I looked into the most beautiful eyes I knew and feel a surge of blood fill my face. 'I'm so sorry. Are you okay?' she babbles without looking up at me right away.

'Sophie? How nice to see you,' Annie says once she composes herself. 'What are you doing here? Silly question, of course I know what you're doing here.' Annie speaks with a breathless voice and erratic energy as she flicks her curls and laughs with nervous discomfort. We have no idea how to navigate this sudden unplanned moment and then there is Emily standing right beside me, looking at us like a couple of idiots.

'Hi, I'm Emily, Sophie's daughter,' she says and she holds out her hand to shake Annie's.

'Hello Emily.' Annie smiles and looks at Emily with genuine affection. 'Gosh, wow, I'm Annie, a friend of your mothers. Well, a friend of a friend, we met through her... from work.

Gee, nice to meet you,' Annie explains to save me from telling another lie. But it is only a temporary deflection, I know Emily will want answers to questions she hasn't even thought of yet and I will need to expand on lie upon lie. I felt my shoulders slump and my heart thud in my chest. This is not what it is meant to be.

'Nice to meet you, Annie.' Emily handles herself like a professional networker and Annie seems impressed with her demeanour. 'We were just going to grab a hot chocolate from the cafe next door if you would like to join us.'

'Thank you, Emily but I don't want to intrude on your time with your mother.'

'I'd love for you to join us,' I say with such abruptness that they both look at me. I surprise myself into a decision to want to spend time with my two favourite girls. How could I not agree with Emily and invite her?

'That would be lovely. I'll just say goodbye to the people I came with and I'll meet you next door. It may take five minutes to get away, they've all had a bit to drink I'm afraid.'

'We'll order. What would you like? Hot chocolate? I know…' I stop myself from saying something that may give us away, 'I remember you saying you don't drink coffee late in the evening.'

'Hot chocolate would be perfect, thank you. And don't skimp on the marshmallows.' Annie smiles I feel myself tremble with a buzz of delight. Emily is looking at me with a curious expression. 'I'll be as quick as I can,' Annie calls and races away.

Emily and I place our order at the cafe, and I go to the bathroom to wash my hands. When I come out, I stop as I see Annie has already arrived and is chatting with Emily who is animated by using her hands to express herself. I approach the table and Annie pushes the seat out with her foot. I smile at the gesture. 'And Mum thought she was going to beat me,' I hear Emily tell Annie.

'I let you win,' I say as I sit down.

'Sounds like you are both competitive. Remind me not to get caught up in a game with you two,' Annie says. The next hour or so goes by in a flash. Emily and Annie are getting on and they have a lot of things in common. I never realised that Emily is quite political, and she and Annie have some great banter over several topics. The next thing I know people are clearing tables around us. 'Feels like deja vu.'

'What does, Mum?' I hear Emily say.

'Oh, nothing darling, just mumbling to myself.' I look over to Annie, who is trying to hide the smirk that has spread across her face since we have been sitting in this small cafe

The three of us walk outside and the night air is cool, it is refreshing. I put my coat on and I see Annie hesitate to help me but at the last-minute stopped herself. I smile and give her a wink as she blushes.

'It was so nice to meet you, Annie.' Emily leans in and gives Annie a big hug, of which I'm quite bewildered. Since when did she become a hugger? 'I hope we can catch up again. You can come bowling with Mum and me next time perhaps?' She flicks a look at me and I shrug with a smile to let her know it is fine with me.

'Emily I'm not sure of that. You two may be far too competitive for me. Play gentle and we may be able to catch up.' We all laugh.

'It's a deal. Can I drive home Mum? I need the practice.'

'Put your plates on and you can drive. But no radio.'

'Thanks. I'll wait in the car. Bye Annie, nice to have met you.'

'And lovely to have met you, Emily. Bye.'

We watch Emily trot to the car which is close enough that I can keep an eye on her but far enough away that she won't hear. 'How did you end up at a bowling alley, of all places?'

'The conference finished early and we had drinks at the bar. All of a sudden someone suggested bowling. I just went along with them.' Annie pauses. 'I'm glad I did. Emily has your eyes and your humour. She's a real credit to you.'

'She's not usually like that with any of my friends. She's polite but would never hug any of them! And never would invite them to go bowling.' I look at Annie's beautiful face. 'You charm everyone, don't you?'

'I'm just me,' she shrugs.

'And I love just you. I better go, I don't want her on her own long, I know I'm overprotective.'

'It's okay, I'm keeping an eye on her. But as we know we can talk all night and I don't want you standing out here getting cold.' Annie reaches in to give me a hug goodbye. 'I'll talk to you tomorrow. I love you.'

'I love you too. Wish me luck with Lead Foot Lulu.'

'I'm sure she's not that bad. Maybe an intensive driving course for her birthday would help her with her skills. Her birthday's coming up, isn't it?'

'It is. You're full of brilliant ideas. I better go. Bye Annie.'

'Bye Sophie.'

I make my way to the car and out of habit I go to the driver's side. Emily has the door locked as I try to open it.

'Other side, girlfriend.' She chuckles as I groan and make my way to the passenger's side, knowing I'm not often a good one.

Emily reverses out of the parking spot and says, 'Annie seems great, Mum. How come you haven't mentioned her? You and she seem like you both get on. I think you're lucky you met her. But how can she be friends with some of your friends from work? They're really stuck up. Annie is nothing like them. She's so cool.'

'Enough of the chatter, concentrate on your driving. Did you adjust the mirrors?' The deflection is not appreciated by Emily but I can't have a conversation about Annie without lying, but I'm not ready to give anything away yet. Emily drives well and keeps her mind on the road in silence and I am thankful for her accepting this quiet drive time.

CHAPTER THIRTY-SEVEN

Sophie

I thought the arguing teenage years were behind us, but tonight Adrian aggravated his sister until his father stepped in and shouted at them; he does not do this often and Adrian took immediate heed. I'm lying in bed reading. It's been a long day with work and now longer still at home. Reading before I sleep is one of the few things that turns my brain off. I love losing myself in an enjoyable book. I can hear Hugo whistling as he turns off the shower and I try to avoid any interaction with him. I feel uncomfortable but I can't avoid it. It's too late to feign sleep as Hugo has seen me reading.

Hugo slides into bed naked and with an enormous erection. I am sure once in the far part of memory I found this appealing. How did I ever find this arousing?

'I've missed our times together Soph. You seem distant these days,' he mutters in a voice lower and heavier, as though attempting to be sexy. Why am I so nervous? It has been a while, months, I think, since we last had sex. I can't remember. Hugo takes my book and puts it on the nightstand and I feel my breath trapped in my lungs. He leans in and starts to kiss me.

He hasn't shaved and I find his stubble coarse on my skin. I try to kiss back but he starts to kiss me with such force that my head is pushed into my pillow. He gropes my breast like a stress ball. Has it always been like this?

Hugo keeps groping and kissing me. His tongue, like a probe seeking an unseen target drives across my teeth and so far down my throat I'm going to throw up. For five minutes, after fumbling about, I feel him massaging what he thinks is my clitoris. His idea of foreplay. Hugo moves himself to enter me and as he pushes into me, I yelp as I am so dry but he takes no notice. It's a few minutes of rocking about before Hugo rolls off me, limp and satisfied. He lays next to me breathing like he's just run a marathon or conquered a harem of sex deprived women. I am not sure if I should cry or laugh at how proud he seems for his manly efforts with his wife. Surely it wasn't always this way. But I can't recall.

'You okay Sophia?' he says through gasps to get his breath back to normal. He doesn't wait for me to answer, falling into a deep, snoring sleep within minutes. I lie staring at the ceiling, watching the soft glow of the bedside lamp casting up shadows on the ceiling. Tears trickle down my cheeks. I'm cheating on everyone. I'm cheating on Hugo. I feel like I've just cheated on Annie.

Annie. When she makes love to me it's always amazing and she whispers to me like an angel's voice from the heavens of pleasure. Asking if I'm enjoying what she is doing and most times, taking time to satisfy me first. She tells me she loves it when I orgasm and the sound I make, with a brief sigh at the end so she knows my orgasm has subsided.

I feel empty. Has Hugo always made love to me like that? Has he ever been gentle? Yes, he has, if I'm truthful. It wasn't always *wham bam, thank you, ma'am.* Perhaps I need to make more of an effort too for this marriage to work. Or do I just walk away? I'm living a lie as a cheat. I am a cheat. I'm having an affair with a woman. It doesn't make any difference if you're having an affair with a man or a woman. It's still cheating. I'm cheating on my husband; on Annie and I'm cheating my kids out of a joyful home life. I need to make some decisions. I hope I make the right ones.

Annie

Sophie and I are drifting apart, but I can't blame Sophie; I'm the one pulling away. I snapped at her the other day for no real reason. I knew she was just coming by for a coffee before she picked Adrian up from football practice. I snapped at her and thanked her for the five minutes she could spare. I've never spoken to her like that and brought tears to her eyes. I'm going to fix it. Sophie has mentioned several times a passion for good food, both homemade and dining out. I'm always interested in what excites her. She thinks I don't listen, but I do. This time I'm going to blow her out of the water. The magic can disappear if we are weighed down with everyday life. Especially when her life has so many weights to balance, I need to bring the romance back.

I pick up the phone to double check Sophie is free on Saturday night. I want to put the smile back on her beautiful face, the smile that makes her blue eyes dance.

'Good afternoon. Mathematics department, Sophie Williams

speaking. How may I help you?'

'Hi, it's Annie,' I say with a sudden hesitation. 'How's your day going?'

'Hello stranger. This is a nice surprise.' Sophie is smiling as she speaks and I smile at this visual as much as hear it in her voice. She is happy I called and I relax.

'I'm not that much of a stranger. I was only away for a couple of days at the conference, but it does feel longer. I'm just checking that you're still free for Saturday?'

'No, it's all still good. Hugo has a work thing on, and Emily and Adrian have plans with friends. Are you making your curry again? I've been craving that.'

'Oh dear, you may be disappointed.' I smile knowing Sophie has no idea what I have planned for her. 'Can you be at mine by about five o'clock?'

'What are you up to, Miss Mitchell?' Sophie asks.

'Nothing. Honestly.' It's a lie, but just a little one. 'I miss you, that's all.' That's not a lie. Every time she leaves me, I start to miss her before she's even gone.

'I'll be there before five, as usual. I better get back to work. We'll talk tonight, and I'll be on time for Saturday. Bye.'

'Bye.' I hang up the phone with my missing her sigh of longing.

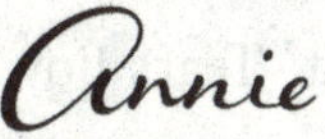

Saturday arrives and I'm excited. The week has felt long and uninteresting, to have now arrived at the best day of the week. I gave Sophie a key to the house months ago, on the three-month anniversary of our first coffee date. I trusted her enough to give her a key and yet she still knocks on the door before opening it. I've told her to just come in and that there is no need to knock. As usual, before five o'clock, there comes a light knock on the door followed by the sound of the key in the lock. I'm coming down the stairs as Sophie shuts the door. 'Wow, you look gorgeous. Is that new?' I ask

'Yes, I found it online. I rarely buy online. I like to try things on.'

I interrupt her, 'I know. You've got a thing for changing rooms.'

'As I was saying.' Sophie blushes. 'Oh, what's the point! I wasn't sure if it was too over-the-top. You have given me no hints about where we are going. I'm not overdressed, am I? Although,' she pauses, noticing the outfit I am wearing, 'I think we are equally attired. Where are we going?'

'You'll find out. I'll just call us a cab.' After a short wait and chit-chat about our week and a summary of the conference, the cab arrives. We muster outside and I turn to her.

'Stay over there for a minute, I need to speak to the driver,' I instruct as I dash over and tell the driver where we are going, and then ask him not to mention the destination. I open the door and usher Sophie in. I get in on the other side and clasp her hand as I always do when we're in a cab; we make more small talk along the way and I'm watching her as we turn a corner and our destination appears in her view.

'No,' Sophie mutters and turns to me with tears rimming her eyes. 'I can't believe it.' Tears flow along her cheeks. 'You're making me ruin my make-up again.'

I'm sitting behind the cabbie and see him grinning when he stops the car and jumps out to race around to open Sophie's door.

'I'm fine, I'll open my own door,' I mumble as Sophie's blue eyes dance. The cabbie opens her door, and Sophie steps out onto the sidewalk. She beams and wipes her eyes of overwhelmed tears.

'I can't believe it.' Sophie pauses, as I walk around on her and the cab drives away. 'I mentioned this in passing. You do listen.' She dabs her eyes and composes herself as I hold her arm close to me. She feels so warm and soft. 'I have been hinting at Hugo for years that I wanted to try this and you,' there's a pause as she takes a breath, 'I only told you once. You are amazing.' Sophie leans to me and gives the lightest kiss on my lips. 'Thank you. Thank you so much.'

We make our way through the large glass doors and cross the restored building's foyer. The lights shadow the walls of brick and wood designs and the smells of the restaurant flow about us. The water boats skim past the wall of windows and Sophie squeezes my hand with excitement. We walk the steps to the lift with a slow stroll as Sophie takes the beautiful building in. In the lift and with our little fingers entwined, we see London laid out before us, the Thames glowing with the city's reflected lights. Sophie sighs as she gazes out the glass walled lift like a child seeing a unicorn. It ascends and stops at the floor we require. We step out of the lift – restaurant one side, brasserie the other. I lead Sophie to the restaurant.

Sophie gasps as we enter the large room spread before us and furnished with at least fifty tables. The windowed wall shimmers with the reflections of a thousand candles, and the people appear to be relaxed and comfortable. Sophie claps her hands and giggles, looking at me with large blue eyes I could dive into and swim in forever.

'Good evening ladies and welcome to Oxo Tower.' A narrow-chinned man appears before us and grins with an unnatural hospitable manner. 'May we take your coats?'

I give him my name for the booking as a young, small-framed girl ducks out of nowhere and takes our coats from us. We follow the thin man as he leads us to our table, where he holds Sophie's chair out for her as she sits. I sit myself and am elated by Sophie's response to my thoughtfulness; I had been worried it was an overstep.

'This is Jerome, he will be your waiter for the evening.' We nod at a dashing dark-haired young man with a shadow beard and glistening teeth who has stepped beside the table. The narrow chin man skulks off back to his pew at the door. Jerome whips out two menus from nowhere and hands them to us like they are large maps we must explore.

'Good evening ladies,' Jerome said with a fresh French ascent. 'Welcome to our modest house of dining, and for your evening indulgences, we have a superb quail with filleted potatoes and a sequined marinated of herbs and leek. Beautiful.'

Sophie is giggling the whole time he is speaking and I can't help join her. She's practically bouncing on her seat. She looks so beautiful and warm and I my heart overflows with love for her. It's the happiest I've seen her in a while. 'Now, ladies, are we having red or white wine tonight?'

'Red?' we answer in unison and this sends Sophie almost laughing out of her chair and even Jerome smiles

'Then it is settled. Red wine for the night. May I recommend the Winchester Malbec, a wonderful 2015 blend?' We nod and Jerome nods in response. 'I'll be back shortly to take your order.' I almost expect him to click his heels and bend at the waist, but he moves off and fades into the lights and crowds about us.

'I can't believe it… I just can't believe it,' Sophie whispers over and over, her eyes damp from laughing. 'You never cease to amaze me. You really do spoil me.'

Jerome returns and pours our wine, leaving the bottle on the table. Sophie, never one to be lost for words, is left speechless, so I order for us both. The waiter disappears, and I look at the beautiful woman who is sitting in front of me, staring at the view. It's just about dusk. We can see St Paul's Cathedral and the whole of the city, new and old, blending in with London Bridge. The night is clear and the city view is not interrupted by fog or rain. The perfect evening. Sophie's eyes are wide, and for the first time since we have been together, she is lost for words. I sit watching her.

Jerome arrives with our entrees. We taste each other's and agree our dishes are sublime. Both meals are so light, you can taste each and every flavour they have added; Sophie cannot resist my dessert. She's not a sweet eater, but it looks too good for her to refuse.

The meal comes to an end but we're not ready to leave. I settle the bill and after telling Jerome what a splendid meal and perfect evening it was, he suggests a table over near the windows, where we proceed to finish the perfect night off with a cocktail.

I couldn't take my eyes off Sophie all evening.

'This has been one of the best nights of my life. You never cease to amaze me. I still can't believe I'm here. The only thing that would top it off…' Sophie pauses.

'I know you have the wedding tomorrow and you have to go home. This was a spur-of-the-moment surprise,' I say, placing my hand on top of hers. 'They're always changing the menu so we can come back another time. Make a real night of it.'

We ask Jerome to request us two taxis as we make our way downstairs without hurry. 'It will be strange not having you at mine tonight,' I say.

'Maybe I should. We could make it a really great night.' Sophie blushes.

'You can come back for a port,' I jest, winking at Sophie.

Her cab arrives first and mine a minute after. We ask them to wait as we say our farewells. 'Enjoy the wedding tomorrow. I know that dress will turn heads; it definitely turned mine.'

'I'll talk to you on Monday,' Sophie answers. 'You have no plans for tomorrow?'

'Just work for a little while. I need to catch up and then a quiet one at home. I'm exhausted.' We both say goodbye, climb in our respective cars and head home across the city of lights.

CHAPTER THIRTY-EIGHT

Sophie

The wedding is something out of this world. Nothing spared and everything perfect. Even Hugo is on his best behaviour. He has a few beers without being obnoxious. I was enjoying his company. I looked at him at one point in the evening and thought, *you can be quite a nice guy*. From where I'm sitting, I see him on the dance floor with Emily. She's laughing at the way he's dancing. *Will I miss this when I make my new life with Annie? Will I still get invited to family events like this? What of Annie, will she be invited?*

The night is over and everyone is saying their goodbyes as though it has been minutes, not hours. I've missed seeing my family. We all promise not to leave it so long to catch up and suggest making plans for the summer and another family reunion. I try to get my family together to head home.

'Right, you lot, pick up everything, there's a taxi rank just down the road. Come on.'

We make our way out of the reception hall with everyone in wonderful spirits. Emily looked stunning in her dress, and everyone complimented her on it. I look at her and smile.

I'm so proud of her. Hugo and Adrian in their black-tie suits. Adrian looks so grown up and his tie has remained done up throughout the evening. I think he knew how smart he looked, and he was chatting to the girls all night, trying to make a good impression. Hugo is singing with his cousin as they sway down the street. I make small talk with Hugo's cousin's wife, Simona. Sometimes it's hard. Nothing compares to when I met Annie for the first time. There was no awkwardness there.

I stop. I can't believe what I'm seeing. I blink a couple of times. *She wasn't going out tonight. She lied to me.* Inside the restaurant we're walking past is Annie, her arm around a young girl, who could be no more than twenty, and another couple, all laughing and joking. *Are they laughing at me? Has Annie told them about me and now they've set her up with someone?* A million questions go through my head as I just stare at the table, she is sharing with three other women.

'Sophie? Sophie? Are you alright? You look like you've seen a ghost,' I hear someone ask, but I'm glued to my spot and staring at the people having what looks like a great night.

I now feel Simona's hand on my shoulder. 'Sophie, are you alright?'

I snap back to reality and play it down. I can't tell Simona anything. 'Sorry Sim, just thought I saw someone I recognised. What were you saying?' Simona continues her conversation but I'm not focusing on what she is saying. *Annie was going to stay in tonight. The last thing she said to me was that she was having an early night. I wouldn't have believed it, had I not seen it.* I try to concentrate on my conversation with Simona, but I keep seeing Annie with her arm around that girl, looking so relaxed.

In the taxi Hugo and the kids are chattering about what a

wonderful wedding it was. In the back of the taxi, I sit in shock. My eyes weren't playing tricks and I'm devastated. What did I expect, though, if I'm honest? She loves me, but how long should she wait? How fucking dare she do this to me? My anger rises, but I try not to show it to the family. I pay for the cab as we make our way into the house, my anger bubbling under the surface. Bustling around the kitchen I make Emily and Adrian a hot chocolate, asking Hugo if he'd like a scotch. He blinks, probably surprised; I never offer him anything alcoholic. I pour him a large scotch with ice, knowing very well he'll down it and pass out. Once he's out I'll be able to do what I need to do; I need to look into Annie's eyes when I confront her.

Half an hour after everyone has gone up to bed, I check on them. Hugo is sound asleep and snoring for England; he will be till morning. Emily and Adrian are asleep as I tiptoe into both rooms and turn off the lamps. I return downstairs and call a cab. I wait outside for it, not wanting the driver to blast his horn when he arrives. I don't want to wake anyone up, especially the nosey neighbours who will then ask Hugo where I was going at almost two o'clock in the morning.

Annie

What a great night that was. I haven't been out with Karen and Denise for ages. I haven't seen them for so long, but once we got together, it was like I saw them yesterday. Loud knocking at the door breaks me from my reminiscing. *I didn't think the girls were coming back, they said they were all going home*, I think. I look through the peephole shocked to see Sophie. At first, I feel a moment of joy but then see the anger on her face. I open the door slowly. In those few seconds, hundreds of scenarios go through my head. Sophie can't be angry with me; we spoke today before she went to the wedding and everything was fine. She storms past me, without a hello, not even a kiss. *He really has pissed her off this time*. I close the door behind her and turn as Sophie paces the floor.

'What's wrong baby?' I ask with extreme curiosity and adding a smile, hoping it will calm her.

'WHAT'S WRONG BABY!?' Sophie shouts. I jump. Good lord, what is she yelling about?!

'Calm down!' I exclaim. 'I don't need my neighbours to be woken up at this hour,' I say. 'Now, tell me what's wrong? What has he done this time?'

Sophie composes herself by taking a few deep breaths. I'm not sure if it's working, as she still has a look of thunder on her face. Even angry, she is beautiful. Beautiful, but a tad scary. 'Where were you tonight? Where did you go?' she demands through her gritted teeth.

I feel my breath catch as I realise that Hugo is not the issue; I am. She has come all this way to my home and screamed at me in the early hours of the morning because she is angry at me for something. It takes a few blinks of my eyes to comprehend this and then I become defensive. This will be a stand-off where one of us will need to back down first.

'Why?' I ask in a cool tone. My arms whip across my chest and my stare lashes out at her icy blue eyes in defiance. 'You come over in the middle of the night, yelling a demand to know where I've been? Again, why? Why do you want to know? You don't trust me. Is that what you're saying? Which is rich coming from a woman who is still playing happy families.'

'I saw you! When we spoke this afternoon, you told me you were staying in. I was on my way home when I walked past a restaurant and who did I see sitting there, YOU! Your arm draped over a girl half our age, laughing and joking; a nice happy foursome, so cosy. How long has this affair been going on? Don't you deny anything to me!' Sophie's voice skips with gasps and tears flow. I am taken aback by her hurt. If I wasn't as pissed off, I might even be flattered.

But I'm boiling with anger that she would accuse me of anything when I have been nothing but patient with her. 'Firstly, do not accuse me of having an affair. You saw me out with friends, friends I have known for over twenty years.' My tone is quiet. 'And the person you are accusing me of having an affair with is their daughter, Merya. A girl I've known her whole life. They are like family and if you had paid proper attention, you would have seen that she had been crying. Her heart was broken because she is struggling with her sexuality. And you know what? Your accusation is pretty rich coming from someone married and fucks her husband while pretending to live a "*normal*" life.' Sophie pales but I can't stop the words pouring from my lips. 'A safe and normal life, that's what you want, isn't it? You don't want to come out and do the hard yards, do you? Not tell your friends that you've left him to make a life with a woman. I'm your dirty little secret, aren't I? Someone who just fucks you and lets you go back to the marriage and play the role of wife and mother.'

'Is that what you think? That I just come over to be fucked by you, and then just leave to be back in my misery…' she sobs. 'It's hard for me; I can't just up and leave—'

I don't let Sophie finish the sentence. 'You think it's easy for me?! That's a joke. Easy? When knowing you go back to him fucking kills me. Easy? Knowing he has what I want so bad? Easy? When I just want to wake up next to you without guilt.' My voice drops and I can't meet her eyes. 'I can't keep doing this; it's dangerous.'

'Are you breaking up with me? Just because I'm not ready to leave yet?' Sophie says with fear lacing her words.

'I'm not asking you to come out. I'm asking you to understand how it feels.'

'You didn't answer. Are you breaking up with me?' Sophie says and her voice shakes.

I put my hands to the back of my head, and say, 'I don't know what the fuck I'm doing, okay?' I sigh.

Sophie lunges and takes me by surprise as she pushes me against the wall and kisses me. 'Stop! I'm not doing this!' I protest as she keeps kissing me along my neck, my shoulders, down my chest. I feel her bite me and yelp, but it is not deep and only in her frustration. But it's hot, animalistic even. How can she make me go from angry to aroused in seconds?

'I'm still angry with you, so fucking angry,' I say as my breath shortens and I feel my legs tremble. I pull Sophie's head back and bring her lips crashing to mine. I have never felt such a rage so full of desire. What do I do with it, but put it to good use with the love of my life?

Sophie has me pinned against the wall like she can't get enough of me and her force is to dispel her anger. One of Sophie's hands is fondling my breast, pinching me hard. Why does this feel so good when it has to be wrong? Sophie is biting my neck. I am going to have marks, but I don't care. Sophie fumbles with the buttons on my shirt, then pulls the shirt open with a squeal of excitement and gasps as my buttons go flying across the floor as my shirt flies open. Sophie pushes my bra up to expose my breasts, steps back and looks for a second, then latches her lips on to my nipple. She. Sophie licks, sucks and bites hard.

Oh, fuck it feels so good.

I didn't notice Sophie had undone my fly and dropped my trousers. My saturated panties follow as she tugs at me with raging hands of passion as her mouth comes away from my nipple; the frigid air hits my nipple. *Could my nipples be any harder?* Sophie slithers down as I step out on one leg and lift the other wide to the side. Sophie smells my arousal as she stands and locks her eyes with mine, then in a swift movement she inserts her fingers in me. I've got no idea how many, but I bend one knee and place my foot on the wall behind me to steady myself as I open my legs further for her.

Sophie pumps her fingers in and out of me so hard it feels fucking awesome. I don't want to come but can't fight it. Do I want to fight it? I feel my walls tighten around her fingers as she thrusts into me harder; her sweat has built up on her face, on her chest, beading down between her breasts, causing our bodies to slide against each other in smooth rhythm. I lick my lips, my head pressed hard against the wall. I'm about to explode. Sophie's other hand reaches up and twists my nipple hard. Fuck! I saturate Sophie's hand with my juices. I tremble and buck as I close my eyes and ride out my orgasm.

I utter, breathless, 'I really have to sit down or I'm going to fall down.'

Sophie eases her fingers out of me. I don't have the energy to take a step and I slide myself down the wall, bringing Sophie with me. My butt hits the cold wood floor and I wrap my arm around Sophie as she cuddles into my chest. I kiss the top of her head.

'I'm sorry,' Sophie whispers as she bursts into tears.

CHAPTER THIRTY-NINE

Sophie

I make my way home as the sun creeps into the dark night sky. The gold of the new dawn waking a new day. I love the morning with all its quietness; the world awakening to a new day. I've been running on adrenaline, but that's faded, leaving me exhausted. What possessed me to go to Annie's in the middle of the night? How I acted towards Annie is unforgivable. I stare out of the cab window as it passes the streets of quiet houses, the people inside likely sleeping in on this Sunday morning. And here I am, carried home appalled by my abhorrent behaviour. I close my eyes, trying not to remember how I stormed past Annie, who was oblivious to my craziness and innocent of all my assumptions. Have I lost her? I make my way into my quiet house, not caring if the neighbours see. I collapse onto the sofa once inside and I cry myself to sleep.

*

I don't hear from Annie for weeks. I go through the motions of my life in habitual routine with many waking moments thinking of Annie. How could I have done that to the woman I love? What was once a beautiful love story, I destroyed in one jealous outburst of my selfish temper. I couldn't wait for an explanation. The look on Annie's face had been one of utter bewilderment. She had no idea, of course, she had no idea.

I arrive home from work on Friday. I left early. Well, the professor told me I didn't look well, so we wrapped it up and I came home. Making myself a cup of tea, I sit there stirring the cup, lost in my thoughts.

'Mum! I've been talking to you for the past five minutes. What's wrong? Are you alright?' Emily says. I jump and look up at her, concern etched across her face. 'And why do you look like you've been crying? Is everything okay?'

'Yes darling, just tired. Let me make you a cup of tea.'

'No, I'll make it. It's the least I can do seeing as you lent me the car. It has made such a difference getting my licence and I do appreciate it. It's filled up with petrol in case you take Adrian to football tomorrow. Dad gave me money for petrol. I didn't need much but I'll keep the change.' Emily laughs, more to herself. I don't respond. 'Mum. You were supposed to chastise me for keeping Dad's change.' Emily looks at me while I sip my tea. 'Mum, can I ask you a question?'

'What if I say no?'

'I'm asking…' Emily says matter-of-factly. 'What happened to Annie?' she said, and I blink as her name is spoken. 'You don't talk about her… or go out Friday nights with your friends. You seemed relaxed and happy when you did. You were… I don't know. Different. The night I met her you two kept giving each other little glances and the way she looked at you… she was listening. Not like your other friends who talk over you, Annie was interested in what you had to say. I liked her.' Emily pauses and appears to hesitate before she says, 'You seem sadder now. Mum, What's wrong? Did you have a falling out?'

'Oh darling, I'm fine. Don't worry. Please.'

'Then what is it? Please tell me.' Emily studies me and again, I see that my little girl is blossoming into a woman. She's so full of insight. I often underestimate her. In fact, I would guess many may underestimate this beautiful intelligence Emily has. 'I know it has something to do with Annie. I know after I met her, you would talk about her more and smiled every time you did...' I do not look up from my tea and feel her eyes on me. 'Were you and Annie more than friends?'

I look up at her and try to smile away a sudden flush of blood in my cheeks. 'Oh darling, why that is a dramatic conclusion to create...' I say, but I feel my breath trembling as I exhale.

Emily nods thoughtfully. 'I guess. I was on messenger with Sally last night and her mum is living with a woman now and my mind just got thinking...'

'Hang on. Sally's mum is living with a woman? Since when?'

'Since about year seven. It's no big deal. She told us a couple of years ago. Everyone knew before she had to change schools because she moved but we still keep in touch via Facebook and text. Why?'

'No reason. It's just that you never mentioned it before. You might have brought it up.'

'It's not a big deal, Mum. What century you living in Mum?' Emily laughs. 'No one cares. Braydon, Sally's brother got a few jibes from some boys, but his mates stood up to them, and they all backed down. They made the bullies look like idiots. You would have been proud of Adrian. It went around the school like wildfire how funny he was. I was really proud of him.'

'Why didn't your father or I hear about this? He didn't get into trouble?'

'Mum, he wasn't in a fight. You seem more interested in it than the rest of us,' Emily said sounding irritated now.

'It's not that. I'm just surprised I didn't hear is all. In my day I think that would have made a bit more news around the neighbourhood.'

'Lucky we're not living in your day then. There's a couple of girls at school who are together. Like I said, no one cares.'

Wanting to avoid the topic of Annie, I steer Emily away from anything that could remind her of her original speculation. I'm loving this new closeness with Emily. I think the moody, hormonal teenage days are behind us and we are returning to mother and daughter again. But not close enough to tell her that her mother is in love with a woman. I need to work through this first. But it's nice to know Emily will handle it well, given her acceptance to the growing number of cases in her circle. But what about Adrian? Will he be so accepting? He may see his father hurting and hate me for it. I'm not ready to face that.

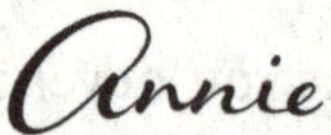

I've been moping around the house for weeks now, as well as been snappy at work or keeping to myself. Maree suggested I take some time off, given it's not peak season. They should be fine. She promised to call me if there was a problem they couldn't deal with. She didn't ask me what was wrong, but I knew they cared for my state of mind. They bought me flowers before I left and I was so grateful; my team is amazing. I'll take them out for a meal when I get back. Tonight though, I'm going out with Jared and Marcus because they won't take no for my answer. Marcus has melted my heart, and I understand how Jared has fallen for him. They complete each another. I love seeing Jared happy. His fears have subsided and is enjoying time with Marcus.

'My sweet Annie, how are you, my darling?' Marcus asks as he wraps me in one of his therapeutic hugs. 'You have lost too much weight. If you lose more, I will be around to cook for you and stay until you finish it.' I laugh at Marcus's concern and I know he isn't joking, which is what I adore. Jared's mum, Gayle, had a health scare six weeks ago and he was so worried, they both were.

When Gayle got the all clear, it was an immense relief. Jared's weight gained and returned to normal. Marcus went home. For a night. The two weeks Marcus spent with Jared was the longest time he had spent with him. They both realised neither of them wanted to live apart anymore. Marcus moved in with Jared soon after and it is clear he isn't living in Daniel's shadow as he had once feared. I knew it would work for them. Jared went to take down photos of Daniel in the lounge out of respect for this new relationship, but Marcus stopped him.

They needed to stay he said, 'He is a part of you, I want them to stay.'

With that Jared pulled him in and hugged him. 'How did I get lucky twice, in one lifetime?'

It wasn't long after that I found the perfect place for them. They wanted to stay in the neighbourhood. A couple had put their house on the market as they were moving out of London and moving to Dorset. Paul would go and value the houses, but he was on holiday, so I went. The inside needed some updating from the eighties, but as soon as I walked out back I knew it was perfect. Without hesitation, I told the couple that I may have someone who would be interested. They laughed at me with polite humour, asking: 'Is that what you say to everyone to get their house listed with you?' It was only banter, so I didn't take offence. I gave them a rough estimate, which they appeared happy with.

As soon as I got in my car, I phoned Marcus to tell him. I could hear the excitement in his voice as he asked me about more about it. I explained it had three bedrooms with room for a small office, and a large open area downstairs that needed updating to the 21st century. I saved the best for last; it had a man cave that could become Marcus's studio. I laughed as he screamed in excitement. Marcus scanned their diary and they could see the place on Saturday. 'You don't think the house will sell in two days?'

'I think it would be a record if it sold in two days,' I told him.

I went back to sellers, asking if they would be free on Saturday for a viewing. They were impressed by how efficiently I presented and agreed. I didn't want them to think I was taking advantage and offered them the chance to get other valuations from other agents. The husband looked at me and smiled, 'I've done my homework, I'm happy with the price and I'm happy with you.' I shook their hands and told them I would see them Saturday.

The three of us arrived at the house together. Norman and Ada, the selling couple, welcomed us. I showed the boys through the house as they fired questions and discovered nooks and had sudden explosions of designer inspirations. I grinned the entire time as I watched them falling in love with it. It was perfect for them, as I knew it would be. We sat inside after viewing the mancave, chatting and laughing, at a table laid out with homemade scones and tea by Ada.

'Please, sit and have tea with us,' she asked. How could we refuse such a sweet gesture? One of the first things to come out of Norman's mouth was, 'So, are you two together?'

Ada screeched at Norman, mortified he had asked such a thing. I never thought the name Norman could be scolded in such a tone.

'It's okay love. My grandson Sean is gay. He lives here in London. Do you know him? Last name Howland.'

Ada piped up, 'Oh shut up Norman, they don't know every gay in the village.'

We all laughed, and Jared informed Norman he didn't know him.

'Keep an eye out for him, he's a nice boy.' Norman winked and grinned.

We left Ada and Norman with a sale pending a few final confirmations. Jared and Marcus were ecstatic about their first home together. They left me at the office as they went off together, chatting about the renovations they were going to do.

*

The boys brought me to my favourite Japanese restaurant hoping it will encourage my appetite. I'm unsure of what I want to eat, but know between the three of us we will order enough food to feed a small army and warm sake to wash it down.

'Have you heard from Sophie?' Jared asks with concern in his voice and sadness in his eyes.

'No. And I don't want to hear from her. She has tried to call but I can't talk to her at the moment. I'm too angry with her. I just… I feel so violated and confused by what she did to me.' I pause, trying to get my words right as Marcus sits next to me rubbing my arm. 'It shocked me. I had never seen her like that. So aggressive. On one hand it was exciting, but on the other, I'm disgusted that I enjoyed it. I'm so angry with her for attacking me the way she did.' I put my hands together like I'm saying a prayer.

'She raped you?' Jared asks, his tone gentle.

I ponder the question. 'She was aggressive, but rape? That's a harsh word to use. I could have stopped her if I wanted. In the moment, it felt like I was role playing. I kissed her back, I enjoyed it. I received a long email from her saying how mortified she is with her behaviour, and she understands why I can't see her. She hates herself at the moment and is thinking about some therapy to help.'

'What about therapy for you? You've gone through a lot in the past year. What you've gone through would have some effect on you. A year where you've hidden away from her life. A year where you've been very patient, loving and gentle with her. You don't think you need someone to talk things over with?' Jared says in a calm tone. 'Go and see Louise. Remember I saw her after Daniel died? She's good, we all know that. Can I give her a call for you?'

'I think I've got her number. Remember we all got together once for a session. She may remember me. I'll call her,' I decided.

'Promise?'

'I promise, Jared, I'll call her on Monday.' As soon as I say that a sense of calm rises and I feel at peace with my world. Although, I have some underlying disappointment towards Sophie. I thought we had something real and I get annoyed knowing what we could have had together and having all this happening instead.

Sophie

My phone beeps again with another message. It's Janice, one of my dear friends, she's someone I've always been close to. I've been trying to avoid her as she knows me so well that she'll pick up on my weight loss, not to mention how I am feeling. Nothing gets past her. I can't keep avoiding her and everyone else I care about. I've gone into hibernation. I'm still ashamed by what I did that night with Annie. I was a different person. Every time I think about it, an icy feeling comes over me and I get teary. Emily has noticed a few times. I keep telling her I'm fine and I'm having sinus issues with pollen or something. My life seems to be all lies.

I take a deep breath and call Janice, knowing the questions that will be asked. She knows everything about me. I love her pearls of wisdom, and she often has some gems. She has done work on herself after a horrid break up, indulged all the self-help books and looked at herself and her so-called 'flaws' to become an even better person. Although, in my eyes, she has always been the perfect friend. She's the perfect person for me to speak to right now and even on this issue. The counsellor is great but Janice knows me.

'Well hello stranger, so aliens haven't abducted you then? I was ready to report as a missing person,' Janice says in her jovial voice. Nothing gets her down. She always sees a positive on anything negative that has happened in her life.

'Hello lovely. I'm sorry I haven't responded to your messages; I've just been busy with the kids and Hugo and—' Janice cuts me off.

'No, you haven't,' she says in a gentle tone, 'I can tell by the sound of your voice something is wrong. You're feeling down; is Hugo having another affair?' she says, not beating around the bush.

'No, he's not having an affair.' I sigh, thinking that may be easier to deal with. 'Or if he is, I'm not aware. He's at home all the bloody time when he's not at work. No, I'm fine,' I say lifting my voice higher to sound happier; failing, of course.

'Right. Saturday get Hugo to take Adrian to football. Leave your car, I'll pick you up at eleven and we'll do brunch. We are long overdue for a catch up and I'm not taking no for an answer. You can have a couple of drinks, relax, and we can talk about anything.' Janice says the last bit in a whisper of conspiracy.

I laugh down the phone as I reply, 'You never take no for an answer. I'll be ready by eleven,' I promised.

'You'll be ready long before eleven, you forget I know you too well. See you then, bye gorgeous.' Janice hangs up before I have the chance to say goodbye. I'm looking forward to catching up with her but dreading it also. I want to tell someone about Annie. I want to be open with Janice, who is the one friend I know I can trust. She will take any a secret to her grave, this I know for certain.

*

Saturday comes too fast for me. I want to see my friend; I just don't know how easy it will be to share things about Annie. A knock indicates she's arrived and I open the door to be enveloped by my exuberant friend.

'Hello gorgeous,' Janice gives me a kiss on the cheek, 'Grab your bag and coat girlfriend, we're out of here.' How could I not smile? Her warmth is natural and it makes me feel good to be around, like a friend should. We jump in the car like we're Thelma and Louise hitting the open road of adventure and talking over each other to finish the other's sentences. Animated as we drive along chatting, forgetting for a brief time as to why I am out with her on this Saturday morning. We head to a place that holds special memories for us. A nearby community where we peruse a small bookshop for hours then go next door to the cafe to pour over our purchases. She knows how to make things extra special, it's like a sixth sense. After some time has passed, Janice lines up some questions for me.

'Do you recall this cafe and the bookstore from our uni days? It still smells the same.' She sighs then turns serious. 'Enough reminiscing, what's wrong, Sophie?' Janice says as she leans over and takes my hand, 'Talk to me, I'm your safe house remember?'

I take a deep breath, let go of her hand and lean back on my chair, looking straight at her. 'I've met someone, or shall I say *had* met someone. I think it's over now. I fucked it up, big time.' Janice raises an eyebrow as if shocked at my statement or the fact I swore. Janice and Hugo have never been fans of one another. I think Hugo dislikes her because she always has a witty comeback when he's being an arse and because she is way more intelligent than him. I tell the story of Annie and all the wonderful things we've done. I tell her everything. When I'm telling her about Annie, I keep everything asexual, never mentioning the sex. I pause, 'Her name is Annie.' I conclude and the sadness in me is difficult to hide as I keep my head down; when I look up Janice is smiling in a wry confidence that puzzles me. 'What are you smiling about?'

'I just want to know if she has a sister,' Janice says and licks her lips as if considering a chocolate dessert.

'Janice!' I exclaim and laugh.

'What? She sounds adorable. We could double date.' Janice moves her seat to get comfortable and indicate her seriousness is coming. 'Why didn't you tell me? You should have trusted me. We're friends, soulmates and I would never judge. Never.' She sighs. 'I'm hurt that you didn't share this with me sooner.' Janice frowns and says with sadness, 'You haven't told anyone have you? You've kept this to yourself. Why? Never feel ashamed of who you fall in love with.'

'I don't know why I never told you.' And I had no honest reason. 'I was worried people would judge me, perhaps. And I was also having an affair, so not my finest hour. It's not something you bandy around.' I pause for a few seconds. Janice, knowing I have something important to say, leans over and grabs my hand with a soft squeeze. 'You may judge me after I tell you why Annie finished with me.' I take a deep breath to steady myself and then tell the tale of how I jumped to the wrong conclusions and how I went to her home to confront her. 'I forced myself on her. I—' this is hard to verbalise as a lump sticks in my throat, 'I sexually assaulted her. She kept saying no, it shouldn't be happening, but I kept going. I was so angry that I didn't comprehend what she was saying, but then she was kissing me. I thought she was cheating on me, ironic I know. I wanted to, I don't know, prove that I was the best she was going to have. This is so fucked up. I've fucked up. I feel so fucking disgusted with myself.'

Janice pipes up, 'I don't think you've said fuck three times in your entire life and I hear fuck three times in one speech. I am privileged.' She laughs to break my upset, but she is empathetic to what I have said.

'Oh, fuck off, you.' And we both laugh. 'I'm being serious here and all you pick up on is how many times I said fuck.'

Janice holds both my hands across the table. 'You're still in love with her. As sad as you are, your eyes light up when you talk about her, so who cares what others think? If friends are going to judge you because you left Hugo for a woman, are they really your friends to start with? Have you spoken to Hugo about Annie and your feelings? Actually, don't answer that, I know you haven't. We wouldn't be sitting here having this conversation if you had. As much as Hugo isn't one of my favourite people, he is your husband and you have to tell him. He has to know how you're feeling and you need to come clean. He came clean about his affair, and for a while you guys were on track with reconciling that. Now put on your big girl pants and pick the right moment, when he hasn't been drinking and explain it all to him. It pains me to say it, but you owe him that much,' Janice says looking at me with knowing eyes and I know she's right.

Annie

I'm sitting in Louise's office; this is my first visit and I feel anxious. I'm not good at talking to people about my feelings. The only person I'm ever comfortable talking to about feelings is Jared, and it's always been that way, even before Daniel passed. I could also talk to Daniel and I miss those days sometimes, but Jared is with Marcus now, so I shouldn't compare. Louise snaps me back to reality.

'What were you thinking about, Annie? You were miles away. I called your name three times.' Louise speaks in a sweet, kind voice that invites you to relax and feel peaceful around her.

'I was thinking back to Jared and Daniel and how it was easy to talk to them and how some days I miss Daniel immensely. I miss them being together. I know that's selfish, and Jared is happy with Marcus. It's like that void has now been filled.'

'Are you jealous that Jared has found someone that he has fallen in love with?'

'No! Quite the opposite. It is lovely to see Jared with a new zest for his life. No jealousy at all.'

Louise leans back in her chair and crosses her legs. 'Do you miss being in love?'

I burst into tears that seem to choke me and I feel the burn of red in my cheeks as I do not cry like this in front of anyone. 'I'm in love and miss being with her. She has chosen to stay where she is and I must move on and not with someone else.' I pause, 'Now that sounds dramatic and I don't do drama, but I just miss her.' I'm saved by the bell as I hear a quiet ding and know we have five minutes remaining. I haven't said so much to a virtual stranger for so long and I do feel better for it. I feel like

I no longer have the world on my shoulders.

'I'd like to see you again in a week. If you want to see me, I'm available after six most evenings.'

I look in my diary through blurred eyes as I wipe my nose with a tissue and review my next week of appointments. 'Are you free Friday? I know it's the end of the week for you. If not, we can make it Tuesday next week.'

'No, I can do Friday. Six good for you?' Louise says as she flips her diary. I watch her wet the tips of her fingers with a sponge on her desk. Her long fingers and manicured nails draw my attention because they remind me of Sophie's nails.

Louise hands me a card on which is now written the next appointment. 'You'll also get a reminder email on Friday, in case you have a busy week and it slips your mind.'

'Thank you. I won't forget. I feel a lot clearer after seeing you. I'm sure it can only get better. See you Friday and have a good week.'

I get into the lift and lean on the back wall as I let out a sigh and say out loud, 'Not as bad as I thought it was going to be.' Just as the lift doors open and a person steps in and looks at me with a quizzical glance. He must have heard me talking to myself and I smile at him. He turns to face the doors as they close and the time spent together is reduced to the floor numbers flashing overhead.

I've taken the afternoon off work. A week ago, I organised Emily and Adrian to stay with Hugo's mother for the night as his father had a knee operation that put him in rehab, so it was the perfect excuse to send the kids to their grandmother's. Hugo also added that it was a nice gesture to make sure that she isn't alone. I have other plans though, and a need to talk to Hugo without distraction. I have a thousand thoughts racing through my mind and none of them helps me to broach the subject. By some miracle, I pray to be able to say what I must and not hurt Hugo in the process. But hurt is inevitable, so I guess I hope the measure of his hurt is not awful and maybe I can get his forgiveness and all this will be our saving grace. I hear Hugo's car pull up and my stomach goes into overdrive like a whole bat cave of bats is fluttering away in there.

He comes through the side door, 'Oh hi, Soph, am I late or are you home early? Have the kids already gone over to Mum's?' Why is he being so nice? This would be easier if he were being horrible to me. He goes over and puts the kettle on. 'Cup of tea, love?' *Oh, fuck you, stop being so nice.*

'I'd love one. Thank you.' I sigh with guilt flowing throughout my body. He talks light-heartedly as he fluffs about making the tea. He often made it a task than a simple effort and I find myself smiling at his innocent maleness.

Hugo brings over his master creation of tea-for-two and sits opposite me, prattling on about his day and what he is working on at the moment. Why today, of all days, is he being nice? I know in my heart he is often a nice guy and I think I maybe focus on the things less positive about him. 'How was your day? Did the Prof give you the afternoon off?'

I take a deep breath. My hands are shaking. Hugo leans across and holds them.

'Sophie, what's wrong? Are you okay?' he asks with urgency

and I realise he will go into a panic attack of concerns, or assumptions, if I do not speak out now. 'Are the kids okay? What's wrong?'

In my head I shout at him, *STOP BEING SO FUCKING NICE!*

Hugo is watching me with a genuine concern, his eyes large and confused.

'What's going on, hon?' he whispers, as another realised concern rises in his mind. My eyes give me away all the time; with him and Annie, both who know me so well.

'Hugo.' I pause. 'I've been having an affair for the past twelve months. Or perhaps I should say I *was* having an affair; it's over now.' I lower my head, ashamed and I don't want to see the hurt in his eyes, or worse, to see no hurt in his eyes. He takes his hands away from mine and I hear him let out a slow, controlled breath. He runs his fingers through his hair and holds his hands behind his head which he often does when he is thinking on subjects that cause him discomfort.

'I'm so sorry, Hugo, so sorry.' I feel tears rising as my breath chokes in my throat. 'It just happened. I didn't go out looking for it.'

Hugo sits there steely-eyed then with a quiet, steady voice, asks the question I knew he would. 'Who is he?'

'It's a she,' I say and it is out. I'm free and the words float between us like in a cartoon bubble. He blinks and rubs his head more with his thoughtful hands. He lets another slow breath escape him.

'Whoa! A she? You've cheated on me with a woman? Now, that I wouldn't have guessed. Talk about a curve ball,' he almost had a sarcastic tone under his hurt. 'A woman? The boys will have a merry laugh at me for this.'

'Hugo, this is about me and the feeling I've always had towards women.' I talked but knew nothing was being absorbed by him as he rubbed and shook his head. 'I denied it for so long because of a life I promised you, and Emily and Adrian. It was all I ever wanted, but I can't deny my true feelings anymore. But it's finished now…'

Hugo interrupts before I can go on. 'How many affairs have you had with women?'

'Only the one.' I snap back, surprised by this question and confused by its relevance, yet when Hugo had his affair, I had wondered if there were more women.

Hugo narrows his eyes. 'Friday nights. Going out with the girls, wasn't the girls at all? You were with her. And she knew you were married, I bet? A lesbian. A fucking lesbian. A dyke.'

'STOP! Stop now.' I smack my hand on the table and feel my temper kick in. He is not going to attack me for being who I am and being honest with him, no matter how late I am at telling him the truth. 'I will not tolerate that language,' I say. 'Did I carry on and call Tracey all the cheap, tawdry names on the planet? No. Please, have a little understanding here. I took what you had done and put it in the past as it was over, and we moved on from it.'

'I'm not sure I can get over this, Sophie. I feel emasculated, I guess,' Hugo says. 'Would I feel differently if it was a man you were having an affair with? I don't know. Have you fantasised about women as we were having sex?'

'Hugo stop, please. I know you're hurting. You are an amazing man and father; you always have been. I couldn't ask for a better father. We have both worked hard to provide a wonderful life for the kids. We have been to some amazing places, experienced so much, but I'm not in love with you anymore. It has been breaking my heart every day.' Tears escape as I say this, knowing that whether Annie had come along or not, this outcome was inevitable. If Annie doesn't want me back and has moved on, then so will I, one day. Maybe not with another woman but living how I want to live my life in the future.

'We need to tell the kids.' He sighs, as if realising I may be right and all the anger and yelling at each other is not going to create any new bridges to happiness. I have a strong feeling he's relieved. I know he has been unhappy for a long time too. 'Are you still coming to Mum and Dad's for roast on Sunday? They'll be devastated, you know that, Sophie.'

'Hugo, please, slow down. Yes, Emily and Adrian need to be the first people we tell but let's you and I get our heads around this. You and I need to be on the same track with this.'

'Are you going to tell them you're a lesbian?'

'Hugo,' I whisper, 'I don't consider myself a lesbian. I fell in love with the person, the gender was inconsequential.'

'Just give me time to get my head around this. Do you mind if I go to the pub for a few beers?' He stands with his shoulders slumped.

'Of course,' I touch his hand with a squeeze. 'You've never asked before.'

'Everything just feels different now,' he says and shakes his head.

'Yes, yes it does,' I say as Hugo picks up his coat and walks to the door. He opens it and stops as he slides his coat on. His gaze is out the open door, looking over the rooftops of the neighbourhood we have lived in for many years as a family.

He does not look back but says with a distant voice, 'What am I supposed to do now, Soph?'

*

A week later, we told Emily and Adrian that we would be separating. We were both calm and united, telling them it was for the best, not telling them why, although I'm sure Emily knew the proper reason. Hugo moved into the spare bedroom that night with little questioning from either of the children.

*

Then, six weeks after, Hugo moved out of the house into an apartment he'd found close to work. Adrian started to spend more time with his father than here at home. Sometimes it bothers me, but Hugo will send him back if he feels he has been away too long, and he makes him call me every night before he goes to bed.

Emily, at the first instance, didn't want to see her father, but I encouraged her to go and have dinner with him on occasion, and she agreed. So, once a week, Hugo has dinner with his children, and sometimes invites me. We want to show them that we are working through things as adults and finding a new happiness with which we can share with them. Well, I'm happy for the most part. Hugo is dating a woman a little younger than me, but appears to be enjoying the newfound freedom from our marriage. He says it won't last, as he feels it's a rebound fling and may break it off with her because his heart isn't in it. For now, he's just enjoying her company and most likely, the sex.

I've joined a book club with some girls from work and we meet on a Friday night, a small irony. I enjoy not being on edge when Hugo would drink. I miss Annie often and my mind reflect on our times; I know I'm still in love with her. But perhaps that ship has sailed, and she has moved on.

CHAPTER FORTY

Sophie

'Mum, I let it go last time, and I know you changed the subject on purpose,' Emily says with a pondering and thoughtful voice. 'A lot of things have changed now. Remember before Dad left, I asked about Annie? Is she the reason Dad moved out? You love her, don't you?' I knew this day would come and there is no way out of it this time. My heart races, as I blush, and my mouth goes dry. I have one smart daughter and she's not going to let it go this time. I burst into tears as months of lies are no longer hidden. I tell Emily she is right and how I met Annie, and how funny she is. I don't go into detail, but let Emily know how much I miss Annie; how my heart aches without her, and how much I love her.

'So, what's your plan to get her back?' Emily asks.

'Pardon?'

'You heard, girlfriend. I know you're not deaf. What's the plan? Are you just going to leave it, and make no attempt to contact her even just to see how she is doing? Tell her what's been happening in your life.' Emily says with a cheeky grin of knowing. 'Tell her you're single and ready to mingle. Isn't that what people your vintage say?'

'Emily.' I scoff at her childish view on the world, if it were only so easy…

'Mum. Please call her. What have you got to lose? Nothing.'

'She may be seeing someone else by now.' I wonder in doubt. My natural state of mind at times.

'And she may not. You've got a fifty-fifty chance there,' Emily assures and hold her mobile phone out to me. 'Please, call her. I liked her too, remember.'

CHAPTER FORTY-ONE

Sophie

Emily gave me food for thought the other night, making me realise I would like to know what is happening in Annie's life, as painful it may be, but it will be an important step for me to move on as I'm stuck; just treading water and going nowhere. I've made the decision to go over to Annie's on my own; taking time from work to leave early and head over to her house. I want to see her and talk with her once more, even if only to say goodbye. I have not told Emily, but I feel she will be happy I have done this. I have tears cascading down my cheeks as I drive to the small house in the 'burbs. I used to find myself bouncing with excitement to get to her, now I am filled with anxiety. I glance in the mirror as I wait at a stop sign and see my make-up is ruined with streaks of it running down my face. I laugh at myself in the quiet of the car and have a comfort in knowing Annie won't care if I look like this. Then a thought occurs in my distracted mind. What if Annie slams the door, locks me out of her life without resolution? She'd be within her rights to react that way, considering everything. I sigh with a feeling of dread.

Driving over to Annie's I'm in a quiet haze of thoughts and memories, finding myself thinking of Annie's nakedness and her softness against me, which turns me on and makes me feel sensations I have not had before nor indulged such thoughts of anyone. I feel myself blush and laugh again with Annie in my mind, shaking her head at me. I flip the visor down as the sunset crosses the horizon and falls into my eyeline, it puts a glare across the glass of the car windscreen, and I squint as I drive. I'm nearly there, and I'm excited, scared and horny; all the things Annie brings into my life with a cocktail of pleasure.

God, I hope she will let me hold her.

I'm jerked across the car seat from an unexpected slam against the side of the car. The crunching steel is loud and terrifying, as glass shatters across me and the car is propelled out of control as my arms are sent aside flaying in horror. I scream, but it is drowned by the car crunching sounds around me. The seatbelt jerks me back and forth as the cars tilts and rolls until there is only the hum of engines and a stillness in the street. And as I try with futile thoughts to comprehend anything that happened in the last two seconds, I find my mind entering blackness and then total silence… one last plea to the image of Annie who appears before me like an angel as I fall into the abyss of darkness.

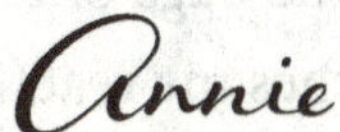

Jared and Marcus have come over for Friday night Chinese. Friday nights I usually have on my own, but the boys have sensed that I'm not socialising as I used to. I'm just getting my head around things after my eighth session with Louise, where I talk about the changes I've made over time. Seeing her once a week, sometimes twice, if I'm having a hard time. The boys were interested to hear about the mindfulness exercises she has given me. I feel stronger, more in control of my emotions. But that doesn't mean I don't miss Sophie. Every minute of every day I miss her, and I fight the urge to ring her. And the love I have for her is still in my heart, none of that has changed. But I cannot change what happened. She chose her life with Hugo and I can't wait until her children finish school.

Friday night is an awful night for me. Well, was a terrible night for me. I don't open a bottle of wine when I'm here on my own, as it only exacerbates the melancholy that engulfs me after a couple of glasses. But tonight, with Jared and Marcus here, it lifts my spirits. Marcus and Jared have been seeing Louise as a couple; Jared going through his thoughts and fears, but everyone can see a mile off they are happy. Tonight, was their last session with Louise so we are celebrating. My phone rings as a knock at the door happens in the same moment. We all look at each other with a freaked-out expression and laugh. 'Marcus, do you mind getting the door?' I say as I stand to grab my phone from the bench.

'Hello, you, this is a surprise,' I answer. I am unable to stop a smile on my lips. 'Lovely to hear from you.' The boys watch me talking. Marcus puts the bags of take away on the table and looks confused as he watches me reacting to what I am hearing.

'Emily. Em. Slow down?' I exclaim. 'Breathe. Slow deep breaths,' I say, trying to remain calm myself. But as my legs buckle beneath me, I realise it may be futile to consider not panicking. I reach for the table. Jared catches my phone as it falls from my hand and Marcus grabs me as I follow it.

'Hi Emily, this is Jared; a friend of Annie's,' he says with urgency. 'Can you tell me what's happened? Annie's fine, darling, she's just in a bit of shock.' Jared is listening to Emily and I can see he's trying to remain calm too. 'Okay.' He nods.

'Where are you?' Jared's colour drains from his face. He shakes his head to shake something from his mind, a bad memory. 'Is someone with you now? Yes, of course I'll bring her. Bye sweetie.'

'Jared,' I mumble with a vague weakness. I was surprised by how the news has affected me when I thought I was coping so well without Sophie.

'We're both going with you. You're not driving over there on your own,' Jared says with warm concern.

'But she's at St Erasmus. In intens—' He doesn't let me finish the sentence.

'I know where she is.' He sighs and glances at Marcus who catches on to the reference of the hospital. 'You were there for me and I'm here for you. But she's going to be fine.' Jared assures me as he wraps his long arms around me. I burst into tears. Marcus grabs the car keys as Jared helps me up off the floor and they lead me out of the house to their car out front. They sit me in the passenger seat, jump in and screech away to the one destination I know none of us want to go. Of all the fucking hospitals, why St Erasmus?

CHAPTER FORTY-TWO

Annie

The entrance of the hospital looms before us like a gateway to our worst nightmare and I stop to look at Jared. 'You don't have to come up with me. I'll be fine. I know this is hard for you.'

'I'm here… we're both here for you.' He looks to Marcus as he reaches to take his hand. I wipe tears from my eyes.

'Thank you, both.' I make my way through the large glass sliding doors with the boys in tow. We seek out the best way to get to the intensive care unit where Emily explained Sophie was being cared for. The lift ride is up three floors is the slowest I am sure I had ever taken and with my heart beating so fast like it's going to jump out of my chest. The lift door opens before us and Jared and Marcus step out, but I am frozen to the spot. The air is caught in my chest and I feel dizzy, but then I feel a slight nudge from Jared, who leads me out of the lift while holding me upright. Once clear of the lift and inside the hallway lit by dull fluorescents I move towards the farther end of the hall where the sign points to ICU. As I get closer, Hugo, Emily and Adrian are standing, talking to a doctor. Emily, with a distracted glance, sees me with an explosion of relieved joy and bounds towards me.

Within twenty strides, the beautiful young girl engulfs herself in my arms and squeezes me like I am her lost puppy who ran away.

'I'm so sorry Annie,' Emily sobs. 'I told her to go and see you. This is all my fault. She was…' Emily says catching her breath between sobs. 'I told her to go. What if she…? This is all my fault.'

'Come on Em,' I assure in my worst effort as I am also rattled by this happening. I am amazed at how close I feel to Emily given the very short time we knew each other. 'We're not going to jump to "what-ifs",' I say with my adult pants back on. I turn to Jared and Marcus.

'Boys, this is Emily.' As I say this, she stands up and wipes her face dry and holds out her hand for Jared to take.

'Very nice to meet…' she starts to say.

'Oh, sweetie,' Jared says in an explosion of tears and envelopes Emily into one of his firm hugs and pulls her close. Marcus wraps his arms around them both and for a long second, they all hold each other and share several sobs. Emily for the affection and Jared for the memories of Daniel's accident that I knew were likely filling him.

After the most emotional introduction I think any of them had experienced, I said, 'Is she awake?'

I ask this while also trying to remain calm, knowing I'm not family and I may not be able to see her. Emily shakes her head with a sad uncertainty as I look up to see Hugo watching us from down the hallway with a curious intent. I can't tell if he's angry or disgusted or both as he looks at me. If Hugo says no to me seeing Sophie, I have no choice but to walk away and pray for her recovery.

Hugo is approaching with Adrian behind him. I notice, he appears to have lost his beer belly and walks slightly taller than I recall. Emily turns to her father approaching and grabs my hand for support. I still am flattered and bemused by our bond.

'Dad, this is Annie, Mum's friend.'

'Hello. I'm Hugo,' he says in a calm, sad tone. He extends his hand and I accept it; it is rough like Sophie said it was. 'I think we met once at a gallery event, but it was a bit of a blur, I'm sorry.'

'Yes, we did meet at a gallery once.' I release his hand and feel Emily squeeze my other. 'Hugo, I understand this is difficult for your family and I can go if you're not comfortable with me here.'

'No. Please stay,' he says with an expression of compassion, maybe even desperation. He reaches out and takes my arm and pulls me with him. 'Come into the family room and I'll explain as much as we know.' Hugo shuffles us along as he introduces himself and Adrian to Jared and Marcus. Emily holds my hand tight as we walk and leans into me. My mind struggles with all this emotion as we move along the hall to the small dim lit cubicle of a room which was furnished with out-of-date lounges and side tables the caveman would have tossed away. I glance at Jared and he gives me a nod; he is okay.

'Please, all of you, come in. Please have a seat,' he says and points to the lounges. 'It appears Sophia was driving to see you. The sun blinded her with glare. It can be awful in the late afternoon on that stretch of road... I guess she didn't see the sign to stop in time...' He appeared to be trying to hold back tears. Emily sat beside me with her head on my shoulder and Jared and Marcus sat across from us holding each other. Adrian sat on his own and looked at Jared and Marcus with confused interest.

'She drove straight through it. She was T-boned by a large four-wheel drive truck. They had minimal damage to their car.' He scoffs. 'Why on earth they needed a machine that big and deadly on city streets is beyond me…' He sighs. 'Sophia's car is a write-off,' he finished with a sigh. 'I just hope she isn't…'

I gasp at his last words and feel an urge to hit him as Emily sobs and squeezes into me harder. I hold her and look up to see Adrian watching us. His dark eyes are narrow and sad, and he seems so alone. I lift my arm and extend my hand to him. He watches me carefully for a few seconds, glancing at Jared and Marcus, then stands and comes across to Emily and I. He sits beside his sister, who reaches out her hand and holds his. I stroke his hair and see a sudden expression I know and miss so much of Sophie. He is his mother's son and he is in pain without her.

'She's in the operating theatre,' Hugo continues. We all look to him in silence. 'She has three fractures in her left leg and a laceration on her forehead. They're going to clean that and stitch it. Apparently, there's glass in it. The doctor says she will be back on the ward soon.' Hugo pauses, looking at Emily, Adrian and the boys. 'Do you mind giving me a minute with Annie please?' he asks in such a manner that everyone moves as if on a dance cue. The boys stand and walk out of the room with a smile. Adrian stands and follows them, and I sense he wants to talk to them yet has no idea how. I will trust in Jared for that one. Emily remains locked to my side.

'Emily, can you go get me a coffee from the hospital shop?'

Hugo asks and she takes a moment then sits up and nods. 'Take your brother.'

'Sure Dad,' Emily says and leaves the room.

The door closes and Hugo speaks while I find myself holding my breath.

'Annie. I know I wasn't the best husband to Sophia.' He takes a deep breath, 'And it pains me to say this...' He looks to the wall away from us and seems to be in a place he is not comfortable with but is opening up to. 'Sophia was happier when you were in her life. And whether you came along or not, we would have gone down this same road.' He moves his hand to hold mine and I first think of pulling back from him, but he is not offering harm, only his open, pain-filled soul.

'I can't blame you. When I arrived here at the emergency, she was mumbling and rambling; she was bleeding and hurting. I thought she was dying...' He wipes tears from his eyes. 'But then clear as day, she opened her eyes and seemed to be looking for someone and then she asked for you.' A tear rolls down his cheek, flowing over the wrinkles and crevices of an aged but distinguished face of a man. 'I just hope she pulls through.'

Then the door flings open and Adrian appears in a fluster. 'Dad, Mum's coming back from the operation.' It's the first time I've heard Adrian speak.

'You go, Hugo,' I say as he looks a bit bewildered, almost fearful of what is happening next. 'Take the children to see their mother. I'll wait here if that's okay.'

'Please stay. I'll come and get you when I can.' He stands and leaves as I sit alone and in complete puzzlement to what just transpired between my ex-girlfriend's husband and me. I shake my head and go to the door, where looking out, I find Jared and Marcus. They come back in and sit with me. I spend the next hour iterating to Jared and Marcus what transpired between Hugo and I. They are as shocked as I am with Hugo's candour.

'I just hope she's fine when she wakes up. No long term issues. Although I know I'll still love her, no matter what,' I conclude and the boys hug me and kiss me with the grace of their wonderful support. In my life there's been times of being alone, and times of being loved, yet in this moment, I would not be able to find a moment in my life where I have felt more loved than right now.

Hugo opens the door. 'Would you like to see her, Annie? She's not awake yet but you're most welcome to come in.'

'Thank you.' I stand and look back to Jared and Marcus. 'Please don't feel you have to stay. I will be okay.'

Jared gives a smile. 'Go. We're not going anywhere.'

I follow Hugo into the ICU as he introduces me to the nurse on duty. 'This is Sophia's friend. I'd like her to stay.' The nurse jots down a note on the clipboard and nods. I sit on the chair beside Sophie's bed and hold her hand. Her face is bruised, and the right eye closed shut with a large haematoma encasing her eye socket. Her lips are swollen and purple with her chin and neck scratched from the seatbelt. Her leg is raised in a rig of wires and pulleys and covered by a cast to the hip. The machines beside her beep and hum and spit out her data which tells us she is okay for now.

I feel tears in my eyes as my breath catches in my chest. She looks so helpless and hurt and so beautiful. I have missed her so much. Her smile and her touch and her gorgeous eyes of excitement and curiosity. Her coyness while playing about and her intrigue into what she was experiencing for the first time. Her fear of losing and her passion for gaining. All the things that make Sophia who she is are all the things I have missed and longed for, yet now only do I realise it as she lays before me at death's door.

Emily is watching me with tears in her eyes. I glance over to Hugo, then Adrian and watch as they nod and begin to leave the room. Emily stays and holds my hand. I contemplate the offer of comforting words while also trying to convince myself that Sophie will be fine. I cannot think of anything to say that would make any benefit to this situation.

'I'll be back,' she says and smiles with assurance. 'I'll go and see if Dad and Adrian are okay.' And Emily is gone; leaving me to sit in the hum and beeping silence alone with the love of my life unconscious.

'Hey you. What do you think you were doing? Everyone is so worried about you. Even Hugo. What has happened to that man?' I offer a small laugh in jest. 'He's being nice to me.'

I stop as I am sure I feel Sophie squeeze my hand. I look into her bruised and battered face and see she has opened her good eye to look at me through her tears.

'You're here,' she says in a weak whisper and her dry lips stretch to a smile as a tear escapes down her cheek.

'Where else would I be?' I answer and know I will never be anywhere else.

ACKNOWLEDGEMENTS

To Mum and Dad.

Thank you for loving me for who I am and for who I love.

All my family: Where would I be without your love, your honesty and your acceptance. Sue, Margie, Hollie, Paul, Amie, Clare, Natalie, Jordyn, Vivienne, Violet, Avery and Penelope. You are my rock. My world. And you all rock my world.

Bridget Berry for your honesty and friendship.

Alessandra Incarbone. Thank you for coming to the Norbreck Castle Hotel that Friday afternoon, and what was the start of many an adventure. And for telling me to save the original story.

Leanne Bell. Thank you for believing in me and my story. Even if after reading some of my chapters you couldn't look me in the eye without blushing.

My little Geordie mate.

Judy Drake. What can I say? We just clicked from the beginning. I love you, and I love our friendship.

H. I wish you nothing but joy, love and happiness.

Emily Santo. A big thank you Emily for your encouragement.

You motivated me more than you will know and I am forever grateful.

Robyn Mandell. My wild, red-haired New Yorker. Thank goodness your dad married an Englishwomen, otherwise my life wouldn't be as bright. Thank you for our friendship, your love and for being you. You're amazing.

Lisa Arnold. Thank you for listening. And listening. Your sage advice has kept me sane, and that in itself is a job and a half. I cannot thank you enough. So, a big THANK YOU.

And last but by no means least, Jannine. Nini. My dear friend. What wonderful memories we have. Over many a bottle of red we have solved all our woes, laughed, cried, laughed until we cried. Our Friday nights. Our Saturday mornings. You are my rock. My confidante. My voice of reason. My sanity. But above all you are my best friend, and I love you.

Shawline Publishing Group Pty Ltd
www.shawlinepublishing.com.au